THE CLOWN
and
THE ICE CASTLE

by

Eleanor Lian

The Clown and the Ice Castle
by Eleanor Lian

First English Edition: January 2025
Translated from the Italian edition, first published in December 2024

Cover and Illustration by Michael Harrington
English Translation by Jonathan E. Harper

©ROBERTO CALVO PRODUCTIONS LTD (RCP)
ROBERTO CALVO PRODUCTIONS LTD
71-75, Shelton Street, Covent Garden, London
WC2H 9JQ, UNITED KINGDOM
info@robertocalvoproductions.com
www.robertocalvoproductions.com

All rights reserved, including translation, full or partial adaptation, reproduction, public communication, and availability by any means and/or on any medium (including microfilm, film, photocopies, electronic or digital media), as well as electronic storage and any information storage and retrieval system. Any infringement will be prosecuted to the fullest extent of the law.

*Be as persevering as one who endures forever.
Your shadows live and fade away, but that which will live
within you forever, that which knows because it is
knowledge itself, does not belong to fleeting life.
It is the man who was, who is, and who will be, whose
hour will never strike.*

HELENA BLAVATSKY

To the five-year-old me who,
sitting at my grandparents' kitchen table,
imagined this story...

PREFACE

What is Fantasy?
Well, that's a great question. I wouldn't know how to answer, or perhaps I'd need so much space between the pages of a book like this that I'd end up writing one book within another.
So, I have a better idea: I can confidently say that there is someone, a flesh-and-blood person, who embodies the very concept of Fantasy in this earthly dimension; her name is Eleanor Lian: a true blend of surprises, emotions, and so much, so much imagination.
This is the first in a series of editorial projects that I have the honor of producing and presenting to you, dear readers; a mix of adventure, passion, and emotions... in a single word: Fantasy.
That's what Eleanor Lian is. I hope each of you can dive into her wonderfully original story and savor every single nuance. Step into her world—you won't regret it.

Roberto Calvo (Publisher, RCP)

CHAPTER 1

Queen Eloise felt the fire of impatience burning in her chest. The dreams she'd had that night had been the harbingers of a brilliant idea, and now she couldn't wait to share it with her child and with the King, her husband.

Careful not to make any noise, she entered little George's room, stepping over the toys scattered all over the floor. As she did every morning, she hurried to answer the lively chirping of the sparrow, Picchi, who was waiting for his breakfast outside the windowsill.

"Good morning! You're restless just like me today, huh?" she said with a smile, pulling back the thick brocade curtains and throwing open the shutters. "Here, these are for you."

While she poured a generous handful of seeds, the bird flitted cheerfully around her before settling down to enjoy his feast.

After watching him for a while, Eloise turned toward the bed and paused to gaze at her son's face, now bathed in sunlight. How beautiful her little prince was, with lips that looked like rose petals, his fair complexion, and those wonderful ebony curls!

He was the spitting image of his father, the man who had made her fall so hopelessly in love nine years ago.

With endless tenderness, she sat beside him and, after softly stroking his cheek, she called to him.

“My love... hey, George... wake up...”

“Uhmmm... let me sleep a little longer, Mom...” he mumbled, clearly uncooperative.

“A little longer? ... The sun is high! Come on, get up!”

“Uhmmm... noooo...”

“Want to bet I know how to wake you up?”

Eloise launched into her best tickling session, and the boy burst out laughing.

The little boy’s laughter was so contagious that soon she couldn’t help but join in. Suddenly, he sat up and threw his arms around her in a hug.

“Good morning, Mom!”

“Good morning, sweetheart! Last night, I came up with a wonderful idea, and I can’t wait to share it with you and your dad!”

“What is it? What is it?” he asked immediately, his eyes wide with curiosity.

“Just a little patience, and you’ll find out! Let’s go downstairs!”

“Yes!”

The boy jumped out of bed, grabbed Ciùciù, his favorite clown-shaped stuffed toy, squeezed his mom’s hand tightly, and ran off, pulling her along as they left the room.

In the grand dining hall of the royal family, King Alexander was already seated for breakfast, waiting for his family to join him.

"Dad, Dad!"

The cheerful shouts of the little whirlwind could be heard even before he entered, and the King prepared to welcome him.

As George entered, he let go of his mother's hand and dashed toward his father.

The young sovereign, ready and waiting, scooped him up, tossed him into the air, and caught him mid-flight!

The boy laughed uncontrollably, delighted by the game.

"There's my boy! Good morning!" the King said, holding him close and, at the same time, leaning in to plant a tender kiss on his wife's lips.

"Do you know what, Dad? Mom said she has something to tell us!!!" George announced enthusiastically.

The King looked at her with curiosity.

Eloise smiled.

"Let's sit down so I can explain everything to you calmly."

Obediently, the King and the Prince took their seats, looking at her with eager anticipation.

"Well, here's the thing... George's sixth birthday is coming up soon, and so is Carnival... so I was thinking: why don't we combine the two into one big celebration? We could host everything here at the castle! What do you think, Alexander? And you, George, would you like to combine them?"

"Yes, yes, yes! That would be amazing, yes! Please, Dad, say yes! Say yes!" the boy shouted, hopeful and excited.

"Uhm... I don't know..."

"Come on, Dad, please... and it's not just my birthday—everyone loves Carnival!"

Alexander looked at his son; he was so much like him when he set his mind on something...

"Do you think so?" he asked, winking at his wife, who, knowing him well, was on the verge of bursting into laughter.

"Uhm. Ciùciù always says so too!"

"Hmm... well, yes, you and Ciùciù might have a point..." he replied, pretending to still be deep in thought.

His son kept watching him, full of anticipation, until...

"All right, you've convinced me," he said.

"Yes!!!" the boy shouted, overjoyed, jumping around the room, waving Ciùciù everywhere, and imagining the costume he would wear.

"I think it's a truly great idea, Eloise," Alexander said thoughtfully. "Especially right now, it will give the people of Iontach a fresh boost. After breakfast, talk to Jacqueline; if we want to make your idea happen, there's not much time left before George's birthday."

"I'll do it this morning. Now, let's eat. To the table!"

After breakfast, Eloise wasted no time and summoned the Governess.

Jacqueline was thrilled by the Queen's idea, and they immediately got to work.

From creating the invitations and sending them to all the inhabitants of the Principality, to designing unique and colorful costumes for everyone, setting up the castle, recruiting the town's orchestra, and selecting the refreshments and George's birthday cake, no detail was overlooked.

Eloise even decided to decorate every flowerbed in the park with candies, making the celebration even sweeter for the many children from the Kingdom who would attend.

She chose to entrust that task to Adèl, Jacqueline's daughter.

"Are you sure she can handle it?" her mother asked, concerned.

"Oh yes, that girl is a real prodigy. She'll do an extraordinary job! And with the help of good Fred, success is guaranteed!

I'll make sure they receive the rarest and finest ingredients today. I want this celebration to be unforgettable!"

"It will be, I'm sure of it, my Queen. Ah, speaking of which, what costume should we have the seamstresses make for the Prince?"

"None—I'll take care of George myself. I want to dress him up like his favorite stuffed toy... but don't tell him, I want it to be a surprise!"

The preparations involved and engaged every inhabitant of the castle.

Everyone was determined to make the party a success, working tirelessly to follow the Queen and the Governess's instructions to perfection.

The enthusiasm was so infectious that even the children pitched in, spreading their joy to everyone.

Laughter echoed everywhere, and the laughter of Eloise and George, in particular, filled the air.

In no time, the manor had transformed into a dazzling display of flowers, colors, and excitement... perhaps a little too much! So much so that, to rein in the boundless energy of the little prince and his best friend, Simon, Jacqueline one day had to come up with an excuse to send them away.

"No, no, no, absolutely not, Mom!" protested Adèl. "If they come with me to the bakery, they'll drive me crazy! They'll eat a ton of sweets, make me drop others, and I won't be able to get back on time! I still have so much to do!"

Jacqueline gently placed her hands on her daughter's shoulders.

"Please, Adèl... just this once. A little while ago, they almost knocked the seamstress down the stairs. Give us a chance to catch our breath…"

Adèl looked into her mother's eyes and gave in.

"Fine, fine!" she grumbled.

She then scanned the room for the boys. "There they are…" she sighed.

They were in the middle of the stairs, playing with two toy swords.

She took a deep breath and…

"Pirates, assemble!" she shouted, marching toward them.

"We have an *important mission* from the Pirate Captain! Are you with me?"

"Yes, Captain!!!" the two boys shouted enthusiastically, waving their weapons in the air.

"Good! Crew, let's go!" Adèl declared.

Standing tall, she swiftly grabbed both swords and raised them in the air before beginning to march, closely followed by the two boys, keeping pace.

At the first bush they passed, she discarded the swords and, holding their hands, led them on to complete the *mission*.

In the village, just as in the castle, there was great anticipation for the upcoming event.

Everywhere, through the streets and along the alleys, the joyful chatter of women and children filled the air. There wasn't a mother who wasn't wondering what costume to prepare for her child, nor children who, eagerly anticipating the games and treats of the big celebration, weren't playing in the streets, inventing marvelous adventures!

It wasn't easy for George and Simon to resist the temptation to join the others in the commotion, but a simple reminder from Adèl about their *mission* was enough to bring them back to their roles as proper pirates, fully committed to their duty.

At last, they reached their destination!

Fred the baker's shop—a place owned by a round-bellied man with a cheerful smile and a kind heart—smelled, as it did every morning, of freshly baked bread and all sorts of pastries.

"Good morning, Master Fred!" Adèl said, the shop's bell jingling as she entered. "I'm here!"

"I see! And I also see that you've brought along two young and vigorous helpers!"

"We're pirates!" George announced proudly.

"That's right, Master Fred! We're here to protect your business!" Simon chimed in.

"Oh... what an honor! Then I'll have to reward you properly... I just so happened to finish making these cream-filled pastries. What do you say, would you like some?"

Fred pulled out from behind the counter a plate with three enormous pastries, so beautiful and fragrant that as soon as the boys saw them, their eyes grew wide with longing. Even Adèl felt her mouth water.

"Thank you, Master Fred, but perhaps it's not a good idea..." the girl began.

"Oh yes, it is!" George declared, grabbing one of the pastries and burying his nose into it. "It's really good!" he said, lifting his face, now completely covered in cream.

Adèl and the baker burst out laughing, while Simon followed his friend's example.

"You're right, it's delicious!!!" he exclaimed, his mouth full.

"Very good! Now, while I prepare the sweets for the celebration, take your time and enjoy them. You too, Adèl—no need for formalities with me."

The girl thanked the man with a nod and, without any further hesitation, let herself be enveloped by the rich yet delicate flavor of the pastry.

When they returned to the park, laden with pastries and sweets of all kinds, Adèl immediately set about involving all the children present in the task she had been entrusted with. Within a few hours, every bush had been transformed into a spectacle of marzipan candies, caramel treats, candied fruit sticks, crunchy nougat pieces, and delights of every kind!

Even the park's little animals seemed curious, watching the scene unfold; especially two pairs of vivid blue eyes that sparkled, hidden behind a hedge...

CHAPTER 2

At last, the day of the celebration arrived.

Eloise, wrapped in a sumptuous voile gown that highlighted her fair complexion, golden hair, and deep sea-blue eyes, appeared before her husband, enchanting him.

"I married the most beautiful woman in the kingdom; today, everyone will envy me," he said, taking her in his arms.

"Do you really have to go check the fields today too?" she asked, slightly pouting.

She knew how much he cared for the land and the people, but this day was so special that she wanted to spend every single moment by his side.

Alexander looked at her with that gaze she loved so much and pulled her closer.

"I'll be back in time, I promise."

Eloise felt her heart race, her cheeks flushing as they always did when he held her close. Alexander pressed his lips to hers, wrapping her in a kiss that was tender and full of love.

It was George who interrupted the magical moment.

"Mom, Dad! What are you doing? We need to get ready!" he exclaimed, bursting excitedly into his parents' room.

He quickly noticed that his father wasn't wearing a costume but his official uniform, the one he used for traveling around the kingdom. This didn't seem like a good sign to him at all!

"Dad..." he said, suspiciously. "You are coming to the party, right?"

Smiling, his father scooped him up.

"Of course, don't worry! There's still plenty of time before it starts, and I'll be back in time. Besides, I wouldn't miss it for anything! You've made such a big mystery about your costume, I can't wait to see you!"

"Really, Dad?!"

"Absolutely! Now, go get ready!"

"Yes, George, go to your room. I'll be there shortly," Eloise added.

The boy nodded happily and ran off.

As soon as he was out of earshot, Alexander embraced his wife once more before taking his leave.

After placing a hat with countless shades of color on her son's head, Eloise stepped back to admire him.

"What a marvel! I'm sure you'll have the best costume of all!"

"Really, Mom?" he asked, beaming.

"Oh, yes. Come and see!"

She led him to the large mirror in her room.

"But... I look just like Ciùciù!" he exclaimed in awe as he stared at himself.

Indeed, he was an exact copy! His mom had dressed him as a clown, with multicolored curly hair topped by a hat that matched the various hues, a painted red nose, eyes outlined in yellow sprinkled with golden glitter, and orange lips. He wore a bright orange bow tie that matched his wide pants, a vibrant green shirt, and a jacket split into green and orange halves with multicolored polka dots.

"What a beautiful costume, Mom! I really like it!!!"

George ran to pick up Ciùciù, who had been left on the floor. He brought the toy to the mirror and paused to admire every detail, playing as he moved the toy into different poses, which he then tried to mimic himself.

"Am I good, Mom?"

"You're amazing! Let me try!"

Eloise attempted one of the toy's tricky poses but lost her balance, falling to the floor in a fit of laughter.

"I'm not nearly as good as you!"

George burst into laughter as well. Overjoyed, he hugged her tightly.

"Mom, let's go downstairs! Dad should be back by now–I want him to see me!"

"But that would ruin the surprise. You know he wanted to see you before anyone else!... Here's an idea: I'll go find him and bring him here so we can all go down together. What do you think?"

"Okay, Mom, but hurry up!"

"Of course, sweetheart, we'll be right back."

Eloise paused to look at him.

"Give me a kiss, my little one, just one more kiss!" she said, planting a big smooch on his cheek. Then, with joy in her step, she dashed toward the stairs.

Patiently, George picked up Ciùciù, sat on the bed, and waited obediently but eagerly.

In the grand park, everything was a celebration of laughter, sounds, and colors.

The large orchestra had already begun to play, and streams of people were gathering from all over the Principality.

Children were running lively everywhere, and despite their parents' repeated pleas to wait at least for the King's arrival, they eagerly busied themselves collecting and devouring the treats hanging from the hedges!

The Queen, stepping out of the main doors, ran into her best friend, Anne.

The young woman, with her delicate beauty and black curls that highlighted her deep honey-colored eyes, was visibly pregnant.

"Your favorite music!" Anne exclaimed as the orchestra began a new song.

"Yes, the same one from when we were little girls! I asked them to play it just for the two of us. Let's dance!"

Eloise took Anne by the hand and pulled her into an impromptu dance. Although she was having fun, her friend quickly became winded.

“Ah, stop, please—I can’t take another step,” Anne said, panting.

Concerned, Eloise helped her to a chair and then gently caressed her belly.

“Starting to feel it, huh? George was as heavy as a boulder...”

“And my little girl isn’t much lighter; you should feel how hard she kicks! Can you feel it?” Anne asked, placing Eloise’s hand on her stomach.

“Oh, I can feel it! ... Hello, Thalìa!”

“Thalìa? ...”

“Yes, Thalìa... Don’t you think it’s a wonderful name? I just finished reading a book a few days ago with a heroine by that name, and I fell in love with it! Think about it—it could be an idea!”

“Thalìa...” Anne repeated to herself. “It really is beautiful.”

Eloise leaned closer to her friend’s belly.

“I brought you a gift, my future little niece, did you know that?” she whispered, pulling a neatly wrapped package from the pocket of her dress.

“A gift, Eloise? Now? But it’s still early—there are three months to go! You can give it to her once she’s born.”

"That's easy for you to say. But what if she's born early, maybe in the middle of the night, and I'm not by your side at that moment? No, no, I want her to see it the moment she opens her eyes. It will be her very first gift!"

"All right, if you put it that way... fine! But I promise you, if she decides to be born in the middle of the night, you'll be the first person I drag out of bed!"

"I'm counting on it!"

Just then, Eloise noticed Alexander's arrival.

"Oh, there he is! Forgive me, Anne, I'll catch up with you later!"

The Queen, as always completely disregarding etiquette, took off running toward her husband, who was trotting out of the woods and heading toward the guests.

"My love! Come quickly! George looks amazing and can't wait to show you his costume!" she shouted.

"I'm on my way!" he called back, quickening his pace as he drew closer.

They were nearly face-to-face when a snake suddenly slithered out from behind a rock, blocking the horse's path!

Terrified, the horse bucked wildly, drawing the attention of those present, who screamed in alarm.

The shouts only agitated the animal further, until it became completely uncontrollable.

It was so out of control that Alexander couldn't do anything to restrain or calm it. In just a few moments, he lost his grip and fell.

During the violent fall, his head struck a sharp rock protruding from the ground with great force.

He died instantly.

But the horse didn't stop.

Freed from its rider, it continued its frantic gallop and collided directly with Eloise, trampling her head with one of its hooves.

With a muffled scream, she too died.

The crowd and the entire orchestra fell silent for a moment before erupting in cries of terror and despair.

CHAPTER 3

Drawn by the screams, George left Ciùciù on the bed and ran to the window.

Outside, chaos reigned as visibly distraught people milled about. Among the adults, some stood frozen, staring blankly at a fixed point, others ran aimlessly, and some sought solace in the eyes of those around them. Then there were the children—some stood still, unable to comprehend what had happened, while others were in tears.

A knot of fear tightened in George's stomach, and he rushed outside, calling loudly for his mom and dad.

When he emerged, the bewildered expressions on people's faces confirmed that something truly terrible had occurred.

His attention was drawn to a group of men gathered at the base of the fountain depicting the previous rulers of Iontach. They seemed focused on something that, from his vantage point, he couldn't see.

He looked around and noticed that nearly everyone else present was also staring in the same direction. So, he moved closer.

Jacqueline, seeing him, quickly walked over and gently placed her hands on his shoulders.

"Prince... Prince George, come with me. There's nothing important for you to see over there," she said, her voice trembling.

As the boy turned his head distractedly toward her, he noticed, for some reason he couldn't understand, that his mother's shoes were sticking out between the legs of the men he had been trying to reach.

"Mom..." he murmured.

His heart was pounding, faster and faster. The world around him seemed muffled and silent.

But the firm touch of the woman snapped him back to reality. With a sharp movement, he broke free from her grasp and, as if in a trance, ran toward the shoes.

"Mom! Moooooom!!!" he screamed.

He pushed his way forcefully between the men ... and then he saw her: lying on the ground, motionless, blood trickling from her head, her eyes closed.

He threw himself onto her, shaking her.

"Mom!... Mom, why won't you wake up? Look at me, Mom, it's me. It's George. Wake up, Mom, please, wake up! ... Mom!" he cried through tears.

"There's nothing more we can do, little one... come with me," said one of the men, trying to pull him away.

George stared at him with desperate, wide, frantic eyes; the clown face his mother had so carefully painted was now reduced to a smudged mask of color.

"Why won't she wake up? Why?!" he screamed.

In that moment, he saw his father too.
Overcome by a wave of furious anger, the boy launched himself at the men surrounding him, trying to hit them all with his fists.
"What did you do to them? You're bad, bad people! He loved you, he always treated you well! And so did my mom! Why? Why aren't they moving? Why?!?"
He didn't care about the answer, about what had happened, about the truth: his mom was gone; and his dad...
He stopped lashing out aimlessly and ran to him.
The crowd watched the scene, helpless and dejected, unable to think of what to do.
"Dad... not you too, Dad... Dad... Dad! ... Move, Dad! Daaaaaad!!!"
He threw himself onto his father as he had done with his mother, sobbing uncontrollably, tears streaming down his little face, his heart... completely shattered.

Jacqueline, with Adèl's help, prepared two grassy beds on which to lay the bodies of Alexander and Eloise so they could rest side by side. The men carefully placed them there, and George, inconsolable, collapsed onto them.
Anne and her husband Louis approached, and she tried to comfort him.
It was useless.

George lashed out at her.
"Leave me alone!" he shouted, shoving her so hard that she fell.
"Anne!"
Louis, alarmed, rushed to help her.
As Anne struggled to her feet with her husband's help, George felt an overwhelming need to be alone.
"George..." Anne tried to say, her eyes brimming with tears as she looked at him.
At that moment, the boy realized that all those people were staring at him, and no one had left yet.
"Go away!!! Get out of here!!! Murderers! Murderers! Leave me aloooone!!!" he screamed, utterly distraught.
The crowd, seeing the little boy so heartbroken and alone, exchanged helpless glances, feeling completely useless.
As the guests began to leave and the servants retreated to their quarters to respect the young prince's wishes, even the sun disappeared behind the clouds.

Little George, standing before the bodies of his parents, felt helpless.
He couldn't do anything but think that he would never again hear his mother's voice or her crystalline laughter, nor his father's deep voice; that he would never again be able to

confide in them, ride with them, play with them, or find solace in their embrace.

They had left him alone.

Maybe it's my fault. Maybe I wasn't good enough, and Heaven wanted to punish me... he thought.

Somehow, he understood there was nothing he could do but look at them. So he stood still, just like them—a small statue facing the gusts of wind that began to blow as evening approached.

From the castle windows, its inhabitants watched him with concern.

The sudden loss of the two sovereigns had left an unfillable void.

Alexander and Eloise had always been kind and generous to everyone, ensuring prosperity for their kingdom. Now, with no one else in the line of succession and such a young ruler, hard times seemed inevitable... but, at that moment, those concerns could wait.

What truly distressed the castle's inhabitants was seeing that little boy, who had just turned six, in such a state.

Some said they couldn't leave him out there, that they should carry him inside by force, no matter what he said, did, or screamed. But Jacqueline refused.

He was like a second son to her. She knew him well and understood that forcing him wouldn't help. So, from one of the kitchen windows, she watched him and waited.

Night fell.

While the cook prepared a warm soup, Jacqueline and Adèl sat at the kitchen table.

Even Jacqueline seemed dimmed, staring at her hands without really seeing them.

"Mom..." her daughter said at one point. "Now that the King and Queen are gone, we have to act. We have to be strong—for ourselves and for George. Look... he's still there."

Adèl stood and approached the window again.

The young prince was still standing in the same position.

"It's ready. Would you like to bring some soup to the boy, Adèl?" the cook asked.

Adèl walked over to her, grateful.

"Of course. Give me a nice, full bowl, Susanne, please."

Guided by the watchful eyes of the cook and her mother, who were observing her from the window, Adèl approached George with the soup and a heavy cloak.

"It's very late. Aren't you hungry? ..."

Silence.

He showed no sign of hearing her.

Adèl placed the bowl on a rock, then took the cloak, unfolded it, and draped it over the boy's shoulders.

"There, at least you won't catch a chill."

But with a sharp motion, he let it fall to the ground.

Adèl, disoriented, looked back toward the window for guidance, but both women shook their heads sadly, gesturing for her to come inside.

With teary eyes, Adèl nodded.

"You're not alone, George. I'm here, and we'll all always be here for you... Just know that no one killed your mom and dad; it was a terrible accident. Come inside when you're ready, okay?" she whispered, gently stroking his head.

Then she went back inside.

George didn't move.

The night passed without the boy making the slightest movement, until dawn, when he fell to his knees and began to stroke his parents.

"You're cold... so cold..." he murmured, breaking into desperate sobs.

It happened then.

A gust of wind, so powerful it turned into a tornado, lifted him up and pulled him away from them.

Terrified, George began screaming and calling out incessantly.

"Moooom!!! Daaaaad!!!"

He tried with all his might to resist the current, but it was useless. It was far too strong for his small body to fight against.

Jacqueline and the cook, drawn by the screams, ran out of the kitchen.

"What kind of devilry is this?!" the cook exclaimed, staring at the scene in shock.

"Get down!!!" Jacqueline shouted, frightened.

George was so stunned that he couldn't even hear her.

The swirling current holding him up filled with snow, turning into a full-blown blizzard.

The storm split into another ferocious gust, unimaginably powerful, which surged toward the two women, enveloping them and turning them into statues of ice.

But it didn't stop there. The storm continued its relentless advance, sweeping through and covering the entirety of the castle, inside and out, along with all its inhabitants, the park, and the surrounding forest.

Everything became frozen and snow-covered, from the vegetation to the people.

Only the animals were spared.

The current finally moved toward the two sovereigns, encasing their bodies in a transparent, icy dome.
As this happened, little George, still dressed as a clown, was also covered in ice, which became like a second skin for him.
Only after the transformation was complete was the boy gently set back on the ground.
George was in disbelief.
Seeing that his body was entirely encased in ice, he hesitated, fearing he had become a statue and wouldn't be able to move.
To his great astonishment, however, he discovered that he could move perfectly well.
"Why am I not cold? ..." he wondered, perplexed.
He didn't have an answer, but deep down, he didn't care.
He turned and, with horror, noticed that Jacqueline and the cook's bodies had been turned into statues!
Stunned, he ran to them, observing and touching them.
Maybe they could move like he could!
But he quickly realized this wasn't the case.
Their terrified expressions made it clear they truly had been sculpted by that icy force.
A thought filled with dread crossed his mind: if they had been turned into statues, then... no, it couldn't be. Not her too!
"Adèèèèèèllll!!!" he screamed, racing into the kitchen.

In the village of Iontach below, people had poured out of their houses and into the streets, struck by the furious snowstorm enveloping the entire area of the castle and the surrounding vegetation.

Everyone was asking what could possibly be happening—such a phenomenon had no precedent.

Anne and Louis, standing at one of the windows of their home, watched the scene with deep unease.

“Please, Louis, go see what’s happening! George might be in danger!”

But Louis, having quickly thrown on his coat, was already running out the door.

More than a few people had the same thought.

Fred the baker, Gretel the seamstress, the greengrocer, and many others were already making their way to the manor to offer help to its inhabitants.

When they reached the gate separating the hill from the park, they tried to enter, but unexpectedly, as soon as they attempted to open it, they were forcefully repelled by an invisible and powerful current.

“Let’s try again, everyone, come on!” Louis shouted, taking charge of the situation. “Our future King is in there, along with many men, women, and children! They could be in danger!"

Fred backed him up.

"Louis is right! Let's go, everyone together!"

The group closed ranks, forming a compact phalanx.

"On my count!... Go!!!"

At Louis's signal, they ran and leapt in an attempt to climb over the gate, but as soon as their hands touched the metal, they were flung back and vanished into thin air.

When they reappeared, each in their own homes, incredulous and shaken, word began to spread through the streets of Iontach that the castle was cursed.

Evilia, one of the village's elderly women, was more certain of this than ever and went from house to house, insisting that if they didn't heed her warning and tried to re-enter the castle, the curse that had struck it would spread to Iontach and its inhabitants as well!

Day by day, everyone began to believe her, and even talking about the castle became forbidden.

Only the children refused to give up, at least at first.

"Mom, Dad..." Simon tried to say several times, "George is my best friend. I can't leave him there! There must be a way to get inside! There has to be!"

Whether there really was a way, no one would ever know; his parents wouldn't hear of it, and the same scene played out in every home. All the children who initially tried to resist were strictly forbidden even to approach the castle or its walls.

And so, they never found out.

Inside, George was left completely alone.

CHAPTER 4

Months passed without anyone making another attempt to do anything.

After a few days, the storm had subsided, but in Iontach, silence fell, accompanied by a deep sadness.

There was no more joy in the streets: no games played outdoors, no laughter, no idle chatter to pass the time.

Many felt guilty for abandoning the manor's inhabitants to their fate, but the fear of the unknown, fueled by Evilia's words, had overcome both courage and common sense. The unspoken, collective decision was to keep silent.

If no one spoke of it, what had happened would turn into legend—a tale to tell to newborns. Sooner or later, even those who had lived through it would come to believe it was just a story, burying it in their memories.

In the great park, everything had turned into an enormous open-air ice sculpture, and the castle appeared as a polished gem illuminated by the sun's rays.

Inside the grand building, every hallway, every piece of furniture, every door, every chandelier was frozen, and as one moved through it, they would occasionally encounter those who, just months earlier, had been its inhabitants, now transformed into true sculptures.

The cacophony of George's footsteps was the only sound that could be heard.
The boy, in his new and eternal form as an icy clown, wandered apathetically from room to room, shattered by grief, his only comfort being his puppet, Ciùciù, now also turned to ice.
As he did every day, he entered Adèl's room and paused to look at her statue.
Standing by the window, the girl had a frightened expression on her face.
The boy gently brushed her hand. Then, standing on tiptoes, he softly stroked her face.
"Hi, Adèl, how are you today?... What's that?... I can't hear you.... I hope this ice melts someday. I miss you so much."
He hugged her tenderly, then left her room, pulling the door closed behind him.
"This silence is so awful. I know you don't like it—it shouldn't bother you."
Slowly, he walked away.

George returned to his room.
It was completely dark there, as thick as a dense black fog.
Sad and exhausted, the boy lay down on his bed and fell into a deep sleep.
"Tap, tap... tap, tap... tap, tap... tap, tap... tap, tap..."

"Uhm..." he groaned in his sleep.

"Tap, tap... tap, tap... tap, tap... tap, tap... tap, tap..."

Annoyed by the persistent tapping, he got out of bed and headed decisively toward the window, fully aware of who was causing the disturbance.

"Picchi! Stop it!" he shouted.

But the robin had no intention of stopping.

"Tap, tap... tap, tap... tap, tap... tap, tap... tap, tap," it continued.

Irritated, George forcefully pulled back the heavy, ice-covered brocade curtains, and in an instant, he was flooded with blinding sunlight, so much so that he had to shield his eyes with his hand.

"Tap, tap... tap, tap... tap, tap... tap, tap... tap, tap..."

"Stop it!"

Picchi continued undeterred.

"Tap, tap... tap, tap... tap, tap... tap, tap... tap, tap..."

"Ahhh, I said stop it!" George yelled, throwing the window open in frustration.

The robin took him at his word and stopped tapping on the glass—only to dart inside the room like a rocket and begin circling insistently around the boy.

It pecked at his shoulder, then flew toward the door, came back, pecked at his other shoulder, and flew back to the door again. Then it dove down, grabbed a corner of the boy's icy clothing, and tugged. It pulled, let go, and tugged again. Over and over.

George was truly fed up!

“Honestly, leave me alone! What do you want?!”

Picchi clearly wasn’t giving up—it was obvious he wanted to lead George somewhere. Finally, the boy gave in.

“You’re so annoying, you know? ... Fine, I’ll come with you. Let’s go!” he exclaimed, picking up Ciùciù.

The robin chirped happily, performed a satisfied little twirl, and headed toward the bedroom door.

At the doorway, it turned to make sure the boy was following, and once certain, it crossed the threshold.

Its little human friend followed, huffing in frustration.

Together, Picchi, George, and Ciùciù made their way through every corridor of the castle.

The robin darted around like crazy, so much so that George had to start running to keep up with him.

Not content with simply being followed, Picchi decided at one point to play a little prank on the boy to cheer him up. He zipped into the enormous library and, with one last chirp, dove into the shelves overflowing with books, disappearing.

“Where are you? Come on, come out...”

In response, Picchi silently glided behind George and, quick as a flash, pulled his hat down over his eyes! Then, chirping happily, he flitted and fluttered in front of him.

The boy was furious.

“Stop it! If you keep this up, I won’t follow you anymore!” he declared.

The robin then perched on his shoulder, let out a soft chirp, and gave him a gentle peck on the cheek.

“Was that... a kiss? ...” the boy asked, surprised and now far less annoyed.

Picchi fluttered in front of him again, as if inviting him to continue following.

“All right, all right, I’m coming...”

And the two friends resumed their journey.

Picchi, confident in his gliding through the long corridors and immense staircases, led George all the way down to the castle’s underground chambers.

“Wait, it’s too dark here. Let me light a torch...”

The boy looked around until he found a torch next to an imposing ice-coated suit of armor.

Pulling out some matches, he lit it, casting light across the space. A powerful wave of nostalgia overwhelmed him.

“Why did you bring me here?” he asked, feeling utterly defeated.

The robin didn't answer; he simply fluttered in front of him, as if pleading for him to make one last effort.

It wasn't easy to move his feet again, but in the end, George followed.

Picchi, moving with great certainty, ventured into the dark rooms, staying within the glow of the small light, and continued his flight until he stopped in front of a massive, heavy wrought-iron door.

Then, turning toward George, he began flapping his wings frantically.

"I guess you want me to go in..."

With great effort, the boy pushed the frozen door open and widened his eyes in amazement.

CHAPTER 5

In the village of Iontach, the cry of a newborn broke the stillness of Anne and Louis's marital bedroom.
"She's beautiful... you've created a masterpiece," Louis said tenderly, gazing in awe at the lively little baby cradled in her mother's arms.
With her round face, big, bright eyes as blue as a sapphire, soft lips like freshly bloomed buds, and thick blonde curls covering her head, she had already stolen the hearts of both her parents.
"We made her together..." Anne replied.
"What shall we name her?"
A shadow of melancholy crossed the woman's eyes.
"Thalìa... I want to name her Thalìa."

In front of George stretched a large, bright room filled with magnificent paintings, blank canvases, wooden tables, decorated fabrics, mannequins, threads, needles, paints of every kind, and brushes.
"Mom's workshop..." he murmured.
He entered cautiously, almost as if afraid of disturbing its essence.
It was the only room in the entire castle, inside and out, untouched by ice. And yet, for the first time since the

accident, the boy felt a sharp chill and hugged himself in an attempt to warm up.

His attention was drawn to the easel where Eloise used to create her works of art.

Sitting atop it was her last painting.

It was still unfinished, but the figures were clearly outlined: her, her husband, and their son, dressed for Carnival, posing together, smiling like in an old family photograph.

"Mom... Dad..." George whispered, gently touching their faces on the canvas.

But then, a sudden wave of anger overtook him!

In a burst of emotion, he grabbed the painting and hurled it to the ground!

"Why?! Why?!?" he screamed, stomping on it over and over, as if trying to destroy it completely.

He was so consumed by his fury that, at some point, he felt the veins in his head throbbing painfully and was forced to stop.

Unable to move, his eyes closed, his fists clenched tightly at his sides, he was shaken by heavy, uncontrollable breaths. He felt tears streaming down his face, abundant and unstoppable.

"Why?... Why? ..." he repeated, over and over, overcome by convulsive sobs.

Picchi, seeing his little human friend in such a state, flew to him and perched on his shoulder.

Gently, the robin gave him tiny pecks on the face to distract him; as soon as he noticed it was working, he began tugging on George's icy jacket again.

Now a bit calmer, George took a deep breath before resuming his journey, following the robin.

They made their way across the entire workshop until they stopped in front of a door George didn't recall ever seeing before.

It was smaller than the other doors, made of thick, polished wood that almost seemed to shine.

Picchi appeared to be losing his mind. He flitted about excitedly in front of it, hopping on the handle with his tiny feet.

"All right, we've come this far, and you want me to open it. Where could you possibly want to take me? Maybe it's a little storage room for Mom's paints..."

But it wasn't.

As soon as George opened the door, he was struck by a light so intense it blinded him.

Shielding his eyes, George managed to cross through the blinding light and reopen them, only to be left speechless.

Before him lay a beach with sparkling, silvery sand, so vast it seemed endless.
All around were dunes of varying sizes, and the ocean, painted in shades of green, blue, and pink, appeared boundless.
"Where are we? What is this place?" George asked Picchi.
No answer, no cheerful chirping.
He looked around, but his friend seemed to have vanished.
He turned back toward the door he had just entered... or exited... and at that very moment, he saw Picchi and the door itself vanish before his eyes, leaving in their place only a smooth, towering cliff.
"Picchi! Picchiiiiii!!! ... Come back, Picchi!!!" he shouted with all his might.
But the robin was gone.
Determined, George ran desperately along the entire beach.
He even tried climbing the cliff, but it was so smooth and devoid of handholds that his small fingers were soon raw and bloodied without ever finding a grip...
And yet, there had to be a way out!
He tried again, and again, and again... but as the sun began to set, he realized that no, there wasn't.
Heartbroken, overwhelmed by fear and an unbearable sense of loneliness, George collapsed to the ground and let himself cry, his tears spilling freely.

All seemed lost when he suddenly felt something wet and rough brush against his face.
Startled, he jumped to his feet and opened his eyes!
Right in front of him, a lively Australian Shepherd puppy wagged its tail enthusiastically, nudging him with its nose and darting back and forth, inviting him to play.
At its sides stood two much larger Australian Shepherds, who must have been its parents.
One of them, probably the father, was truly enormous, with bright hazel eyes that gave him a deep, protective gaze. The other, smaller and with soft blue eyes, could only be the mother.
They, too, wagged their tails in a friendly manner and, following the puppy's lead, tried to involve the newcomer in their play.
"I don't feel like playing... it's cold, and I need to find a place to sleep."
The boy began walking, and the little family followed him.

At Anne and Louis's home, Anne turned over the package Eloise had given her for her daughter in her hands.
It was meant to be Thalìa's very first gift, but she hadn't yet had the heart to open it.
She felt guilty toward her friend.

George was trapped inside the castle, and there was no way to get him out or even check on how he was doing.

Rumors circulated—some said that at night, the wind carried the desperate cries of a child. Others claimed a monster dressed in ice had been seen wandering the castle grounds beyond the iron gates. Still, others insisted that all the castle's inhabitants had frozen to death and that not a single soul had survived.

Whatever the truth, after Thalìa's birth, Anne had tried to return to the manor. But the same strange phenomenon that had happened to her fellow villagers occurred to her as well. When she attempted to force the gate open, she vanished and reappeared back at home.

She hadn't given up.

She tried again and again... but nothing worked. The result was always the same, and eventually, she gave up.

"I wish you were still here..." she murmured.

Then, she began unwrapping the gift.

It was a music box. Inside was a tiny doll—the exact miniature of Thalìa!

"And how did you know my daughter would look exactly like this?" she asked in astonishment.

She placed it on the nightstand beside the cradle and wound it up. Their favorite song filled the air, and the baby seemed to drift into a deep sleep.

A tear rolled down Anne's face.

CHAPTER 6

With no sovereigns left, the citizens of Iontach had decided to entrust the governance of the kingdom to Father Angelo, the village priest.

He was a righteous, balanced man, uninterested in wealth but deeply committed to the well-being of his people. Under his guidance, despite the lingering shadow of the events on the hill, the village continued to prosper.

Time passed quickly.

Thalìa, now eight years old, had become a cheerful child, bursting with an unstoppable zest for life, curiosity, imagination, and boundless energy.

There wasn't a day she didn't race along the streets of Iontach, often bumping into her fellow villagers and earning their disgruntled remarks.

It was a Saturday morning when the girl burst like a whirlwind into Fred the baker's shop, making the little bell jingle merrily.

Inside were two customers—two stern, sour-faced, unattractive, and gossip-prone women who immediately wrinkled their noses upon seeing her.

Not so for the good baker, who adored his young visitor.

"Goooood morning, Freeeed!!!" Thalìa exclaimed, standing on tiptoes to lean on the counter.

"Good morning, little one! Where are you off to in such a hurry?" he asked, amused, though he already knew the answer that would come as predictably as every Saturday.

"To see you, my dear Fred! I came to get bread for Mama! And also some of those delicious pastries that only you know how to make..."

Chuckling under his mustache, the man reached toward the refrigerated counter. That morning, he had set aside one of her favorite pastries: a delicious, giant, and soft cream-filled choux pastry, stuffed like a little sandwich and topped with an inviting sprinkling of sugar crystals.

"You little flatterer... here's your pastry, take it," Fred said, handing it to her, his thick mustache twitching with curiosity for her reaction.

Thalìa wasn't one for formalities.

She hadn't even finished muttering her "thank you" before she had buried her face into the pastry, smearing cream all over her nose, mouth, and cheeks, making Fred burst out laughing.

"It's so good..." she mumbled, her eyes dreamy with delight.

The two women could no longer hold back.

"A young lady like you should be a little more refined and polite, don't you think?"

"Polite... Did you see how she barged in? And what on earth do you have to be so cheerful about this early in the morning?"

"What she has, Gertrude, is something an old witch like you will never have again—youth!" Fred shot back.

"How dare you... You rude, walrus-looking bumpkin!"

Fred erupted into laughter, his warm, hearty laugh filling the shop.

"You asked for it, my dear. Here you go, little one, your things are ready," he added, handing a bag to Thalìa.

"Thanks, Fred!"

After swallowing the last bite of pastry, she wiped her face with her hand, grabbed the bag, left some coins on the counter, and, pulling a face at the two old hags, dashed out of the shop as quickly as she had entered.

The morning was still young, and Thalìa had no intention of heading home just yet.

She decided instead to make her way to the central square of the village.

On Saturday mornings, most of the children in Iontach usually gathered there, making it the perfect time to play and have some fun.

As soon as she arrived, she saw two groups: one was playing marbles, and the other was playing cards.

The card-playing group, led by that troublemaker Francis—a chubby boy with a perpetually menacing glare—didn't appeal to her at all. So, she approached the marble group, which consisted of Alice and Thomas, two kids slightly older than her, and little Boris, a six-year-old boy.

"Hey, hi! Want to play something a bit more fun?" she suggested.

"Like what?" Thomas asked, looking at her skeptically.

"Tag!" she replied enthusiastically.

Alice wasn't on board.

"You'll get sweaty..." she retorted.

"But it's fun! Isn't that the most important thing?"

"Thalìa's right, I'm in!" Boris declared, standing up quickly and taking her hand.

"You're not playing! Mom will yell at me if you do. Sit down!" Thomas ordered firmly.

The little brother reluctantly obeyed.

"Then how about playing ball?" Thalìa suggested again. "If we play without overdoing it... we won't sweat too much..."

Boris, excited again, looked hopefully at his brother, but once more, his enthusiasm was quickly dashed.

"No," Thomas declared again.

"But why not?!?" Thalìa asked, exasperated.

"Because no!" Alice snapped back. "It's always the same story with you. You show up while we're already playing and expect us to change the game! Is it possible you don't like any of the games we play?"

"They're boring..."

"Not to us. Look, if you want to play marbles, fine. If not, go play with someone else!"

Thalìa was about to respond when Francis approached her from behind.

"Alice is right, but she's being way too nice. Why don't you just leave?"

Thc words hit Thalìa hard.

"Why?!... I just want to play."

"Not with us. Leave. We don't want you here," he said harshly, towering over her with his bulk.

Thalìa took a step back to look him in the eyes, then exploded.

"You're nothing but bullies! You don't understand anything! I hate you! I hate all of you!" she yelled, her voice breaking.

Boris hugged her legs.

"No... don't say that. Hating is bad. I like you, don't be sad."

She looked at him and gently stroked his head, a gesture that helped her calm down a little and regain a proud, resolute look as she turned back to the others.

"I'm not the one missing out," she said calmly, locking eyes with Francis. "Fine, I'll play by myself. I'll have way more fun that way."

She managed to say it confidently, but inside, she felt a painful knot forming in her stomach.
Without lingering any longer, she bolted away, just as fast as she had arrived, but this time with her head down so no one could see that she couldn't stop crying.

The sadness of being rejected once again slowly turned into anger as Thalìa wiped her tears away, walking briskly.
When she arrived home, she couldn't stop herself from slamming the door.
"I'm back!"
"I noticed..." Anne muttered almost to herself, drying her hands on a dish towel.
The woman turned off the faucet, leaving the vegetables in the basin, and went to her daughter.
Thalìa, sitting on the couch, hugged her legs tightly, her face buried in her knees.
Anne approached her and gently lifted her face.
"You've been crying. What happened?"
"No one wants to play with me!" she sobbed.
As Thalìa vented, once again calling the other children in the village boring, sleepy fossils on the verge of old age, Anne couldn't help but feel sorry for her.
She knew how much her daughter loved playing tag and inventing exciting scenarios where she could become a

sword-wielding pirate or an adventurous princess searching for treasure. Her little adventurer was so imaginative, and Anne understood her well—she had inherited it all from her! Anne still remembered the wild races she and Eloise used to have at that same age. She knew perfectly well how special it was to share such fun with friends.

However, ever since that unfortunate event eight years ago, it seemed the adults in the village had let themselves be consumed by anxiety and fear. Their overprotectiveness had stifled their children's imagination.

Anne was well aware that this attitude wasn't likely to change anytime soon.

"Are you listening, Mom?" the girl asked, snapping her out of her thoughts.

"Of course... But, sweetheart, if the other children enjoy playing games different from the ones you love, you can't really blame them, can you?"

"But they can't blame me either!"

"Of course, they can't blame you either. But you're the one who tried to impose your games while they were already playing... isn't that right?"

"Their games were boring!"

"To you."

"Yeah. So, there's only one solution..." the girl replied slyly.

Anne looked at her, waiting, already knowing where this was headed.

"...go play ball alone in the fields... ?!" Thalìa suggested, a bit hesitant but hopeful.

Anne couldn't hold back a smile.

"Alright, little trickster! You can go after lunch."

Thalìa jumped to her feet, overjoyed, and hugged her tightly.

"Thank you! I love you sooooo much!!!... Yummm, what's for lunch? I'm starving...!"

Anne watched her trot into the kitchen and, shaking her head fondly, followed her.

CHAPTER 7

George's skill at skipping stones across the water was unmatched! Now fourteen, it had become one of his favorite pastimes.

The years had passed without anything changing. Picchi hadn't returned, the door hadn't reappeared, the three dogs didn't seem to have aged a single day, Ciùciù remained a puppet of ice, and George was still wrapped in that icy clown outfit, which had become, for him, like a second skin.

The only difference was his heart, which seemed to have quieted, beating less angrily and more serenely.

Time had calmed him.

George had learned not just to survive, but to live—for himself and for the three dogs that had chosen him. For them, he had learned to build a raft and face the sea to fish. He had learned to light a fire and cook. He had discovered that, not far from the beach, there was a small oasis where fruit trees, berries, and wild vegetables grew.

It was there, after living for a long time in a damp cave nestled into the large cliff, that he built his small home.

His days were a solitary cycle of mostly repetitive tasks and situations. Afraid of forgetting how to speak, George often had long conversations with his canine friends, even if the only responses he got were barks and loving gazes. These friends now had names: Jo, Alex, and Elly.

Little Jo, in particular, had boundless energy, and for him, any excuse was a good one to play. His favorite game was fetch.

That afternoon, Jo spotted a small stick washed ashore by the tide. Overjoyed, he ran to grab it and brought it to George. But George wasn't in the mood to play.

The night before, he had dreamed of that distant day of the accident. It had been a strange, muffled dream; a dream of screams, cries, blood, joyous laughter turning into the cackle of a wicked clown, and then an unbearable cacophony of tears, harmonious music morphing into distorted, dissonant sounds, neighing, ice statues, empty stares, more neighing, hooves on grass, gusts of wind, his father's head on the stone, a snowstorm, his mother's head under the hooves, and again blood. So much blood—too much blood.

He had woken up drenched in sweat and hadn't been able to think of anything else since.

Jo bounced around in front of him with his stick, trying to capture his attention, but George seemed so dazed that Elly and Alex started barking loudly.

Snapping out of his stupor, he looked at them quizzically. Then he noticed little Jo, who, realizing he had finally caught

George's attention, had placed the stick at his feet and was barking, as if inviting him to pick it up and throw it.

"Still with the stick game, Jo?"

The little dog barked enthusiastically, spinning around to chase his tail. Then, flopping onto his back, he froze with his paws in the air and his tongue lolling out, staring at George.

"Alright... but just once, okay?" George said with a smile.

The little dog wagged his tail and barked happily, standing at attention to watch closely where George would throw the stick.

As soon as George threw it, Jo dashed off, ran, grabbed the stick, and proudly, confidently brought it back.

George had already forgotten about the stick; seated on the sand, he was absentmindedly watching the gentle waves break against the shore.

Jo gave him a quick lick on his icy cheek, then barked again to regain his attention.

"Enough, Jo. I don't feel like playing anymore."

The puppy wasn't ready to give up and barked again.

Annoyed, George picked up the stick and, this time, threw it into the water.

Jo was over the moon! He wagged his little rear end while, with ears perked and his sharp eyes focused, he scanned the waves for the stick. Confident, he dove into a specific spot and, in no time, resurfaced with his prize in his mouth!

He dropped it in George's lap, but... nothing, no reaction. So, he tugged at the hem of George's jacket.

It was so cold that the little dog whimpered. Determined to get George's attention, Jo started hopping around again.

Still nothing.

Alex rushed to his rescue. Grabbing the stick in his mouth, he offered it to his son, but Jo refused to play. At that moment, he didn't want to play with his dad; he wanted to play with his best friend, with George... who wasn't paying him any attention.

Sad and dejected, Jo curled up next to him.

Alex and Elly, noticing their pup's distress, tried to cheer him up with affectionate nudges. When that didn't work, they stood in front of George and barked at him indignantly.

"Oh, come on, it's not my fault. I can't spend all my days playing!" George tried to defend himself, avoiding their gaze.

Alex and Elly then moved closer to Jo and curled up beside him.

Alex howled at the sky, and Elly lovingly licked him. Little by little, the puppy surrendered peacefully to his mother's affection and his father's reassuring presence.

At Alex's howl, George turned to look and was captivated by the scene.

He couldn't help but think of when he was as small as Jo, being tossed into the air by his dad, hugged tightly, and showered with kisses by his mom.

He felt an aching sense of loss.

That was the image of a family.

"Family."

Something he would never have again.

Before he could stop it, a solitary tear rolled down his cheek.

CHAPTER 8

Finally, the early afternoon arrived, and Thalìa's eager wait was over.

The little girl grabbed her favorite ball and headed for the door.

"I'm off!" she shouted excitedly, slamming the door behind her.

Then, she dashed down the empty alleyway.

"Be careful!" her mother called after her.

In vain, because Thalìa was already far away, lost in the thousands of extraordinary and ever-new adventures racing through her mind.

So vivid were her thoughts that, at one point, she stopped in the middle of the street as if struck by an idea more intense than the rest.

"Maybe I should..."

She glanced around, spotted an enormous flower pot, and, cautiously—almost as if she feared someone was watching—she hid the ball inside it.

Then, as quick as ever, she darted off in the opposite direction from the one she had initially taken.

As she briskly walked through the alleys of the village toward the vast valley, Thalìa noticed a window opening.

Quick as a flash, she ducked behind a small table and waited. A housewife retrieved one of the dishcloths hanging out to dry and went back inside.

Thalìa waited a few more moments. Then, ensuring the housewife wouldn't reappear and that the street was empty of anyone who might see her, she quietly crept under the windowsill and darted toward the end of the alley, turning into the next one.

There, she found two drunks, utterly intoxicated.

One was sitting on a step, laughing heartily, while the other was gleefully gulping from a large jug of wine.

Both of them stared at her.

"Hey, aren't you Louis's daughter?" asked the laughing drunk, amused.

"Me? Uh... yes, I mean, no... I just look like her, yeah, yeah, people always say that. But... but I'm not her."

"Of course she's not!" exclaimed the wine-drinking companion, convinced. "Can't you see? She's got red hair!"

"Red?" asked the other, perplexed, as he clearly saw her hair shining like the midday sun.

Thalìa seized the opportunity.

"Yes, red. Don't you see? People have been telling me since I was little that I look like I was born in a field of carrots... but I like it! My hair is really pretty, don't you think?"

The drunk who saw her hair as blond stopped laughing and widened his eyes.

"Red, you say... I guess I'm drunk, but not drunk enough. Hand me the jug; I want to drink some more!" he said to his friend, trying to snatch the wine.

The latter wasn't having it.

"Hey, let go, it's mine!"

"No, it's mine!"

"I said it's mine!"

The two men, now completely oblivious to Thalìa's presence, started brawling in earnest. With a sly smile and a sigh of relief, she quietly slipped away, weaving through one alley, then another, and yet another, until she finally caught sight of the fields at the end of a completely deserted lane. She broke into a wild sprint.

Leaving the village behind, she found herself facing a vast clearing dotted with cultivated fields, crossed by a cobblestone path that led directly toward the hill where the ice castle stood.

Without hesitation, she took the path.

The steeper the path became and the closer it brought her to the manor, the faster Thalìa quickened her pace.

She couldn't wait to reach the top—she felt euphoric!

Her excitement turned to pure astonishment when, just a few meters from her destination, she noticed that the sun's rays, striking the castle's icy surface, created the most dazzling rainbow she had ever seen!

"Woooooow!!! It's magnificent! This must be the Realm of Dreams!" she exclaimed, stepping forward in awe.

Standing before the enormous wrought iron gate, she peered through its intricate designs and saw a snowy park illuminated partly by the sun and partly by the rainbow. It was enchanting.

She tried pushing the gate to enter, but it wouldn't budge. So, she sat down in front of it, continuing to marvel at the sight within.

Everything—from the trees to the bushes—was covered in a soft layer of snow that sparkled magically under the sunlight. It looked motionless, like a postcard frozen in time.

Her awestruck gaze shifted toward the castle...

"This place is so beautiful... it feels like I'm in a fairytale," she whispered. "Dear Castle, I want to dedicate a song to you."

Thalìa stood up and pulled out the music box her mother had given her when she was born.

Now, the little girl inside the box was no longer a newborn. She was the same age as Thalìa and identical to her, even in her clothing.

In her current position, she seemed to be dancing.

Thalìa searched for the button at the base of the music box and pressed it.

"Here... This, dear Castle, is for you..."

A celestial melody filled the air.

Unable to resist, Thalìa began to twirl.

She had never felt so free and fulfilled as she did in that moment!

"I wish it could always be like this, Castle! How I'd love to run without constantly being scolded by someone! It would be so amazing to live a thousand adventures! I want to travel to far-off worlds, gallop on a fast and mighty steed, wield a sword, and fight all the enemies in the world! And maybe... yes, even set sail on the open sea!"

As Thalìa danced, eagerly sharing her dreams with her new friend, it seemed as though the snow and ice around her began to shine more and more brightly.

Before long, as if enchanted by the music of the music box, all the animals from the nearby forest gathered around her. Butterflies, birds, horses, cats, dogs, squirrels, deer, and foxes—all came to the gate and joined her in an angelic dance.

A tiny, all-white kitten climbed onto the girl's shoulder.

Surprised, she picked it up and, holding it close as though it were an imaginary knight, led it in her dance.

Finally, the music from the box came to an end.

“The day I gain my freedom, no one will ever be able to take it away from me again, little one...” she said, a hint of melancholy in her voice, before returning the kitten to its mother, who purred at her from inside the great park.
All the animals watched her with curiosity.
"Thank you for playing with me... It was nice to play with someone... for once!"
Each with their own sound, they bid her farewell, then turned and disappeared from her sight.
Thalìa cast one last glance at the manor and, feeling content, made her way back to the village.

As she walked, the little girl kept thinking about that marvelous place, which she could so rarely manage to visit.
In her imagination, it always belonged to a parallel dimension.
She dreamed of what it might be like to enter and asked herself countless questions about its inhabitants. Had they really been frozen? And what had become of the young prince her parents had once spoken of, but whom no one seemed willing to remember anymore? Could he have turned into a snowman or a statue of ice, perhaps now part of the garden? Or maybe he had transformed into a magical creature that appeared only at night to protect the village, unbeknownst to everyone!

Whatever the truth, she hoped she would meet him one day... but every time she managed to slip past her villagers' watchful eyes and reach the castle, he was never there.

Instead, there were always plenty of animals, and Thalìa often wondered how it was possible that they weren't frozen. Could it all have been just a legend—that the inhabitants had turned into ice, like the castle itself? But if that were the case, what had happened to them, and, most importantly, why had the snow never melted in all those years?

Without even realizing it, Thalìa found herself standing before the imposing wooden door of a small yellow house located right in the village's central square.

Resolutely, she looked at it, then knocked.

From inside came the voice of a woman.

"Who is it?"

"It's me, Aunt Beth. Thalìa. Will you open up?"

A hurried sound of footsteps approached the door.

"My sweet child!" the woman exclaimed, opening it.

She was a woman not exactly young but rather fit, with thick silver hair gathered in an elegant bun.

"... Look at you, all sweaty! Come on, come inside and dry off. In the meantime, I'll prepare you a snack."

Thalìa threw her arms around her aunt's neck and gave her a noisy kiss on the cheek.

"Thanks, Auntie! Do you have those delicious peanut cookies you always make for Uncle?"
"Of course, you little glutton! Now go wash your hands and put a towel around your neck first—quickly!"
"Yes, ma'am!" the girl said, snapping to attention like a little soldier before disappearing into the bathroom.

When she returned to the kitchen a short while later, she found a giant glass of fresh milk and an entire plate of her favorite cookies waiting for her!
With her usual enthusiasm, she dove in, devouring them with delight.
"Slow down! Not so fast, or you'll make yourself sick!"
"Impossible, they're too good! Yum..."
In no time, the cookies were gone.
Thalìa, having gulped down the glass of milk, wiped her mouth with her sleeve and slumped back in her chair, satisfied.
"My dear niece... you should be a little more refined. After all, you're a young lady."
"So what? Girls aren't mummies!" declared the girl, brandishing her spoon and jumping up on her chair.
"One day, I'll board a giant pirate ship, become its Captain, and fight off all my enemies, defeating them one by one!"

She was so enthusiastic that she lost her balance, and only her aunt's quick reflexes saved her from a painful crash to the floor.
"Be careful!" the woman exclaimed in alarm, catching her just in time.
Thalìa burst into laughter and hugged her tightly.
"With an attendant like you, I feel as safe as if I were on a throne!"
"Attendant to whom, young lady? As your aunt, I should be sitting *next to you*, not playing your servant! Anyway, now that you're full, my adventurous pirate niece, tell me: what brings you here?"
Thalìa blushed, feeling caught off guard.
"Um... uh... well, I was wondering... What do you know about the castle's story?"
Aunt Beth's expression turned serious immediately.
"Castle? What castle?"
"What do you mean, what castle? The ice castle, of course!"
"That question again... Perhaps I wasn't clear enough last time. You must not concern yourself with that story, do you understand? Ever!"
"At least explain why! No one will talk about it! What's so terrible locked away in that place? How can it be so dangerous?! It's beautiful, full of animals—it looks magical!"

"It's not magical—it's cursed!" Aunt Beth shouted, losing control. "Listen, I've already told you more than enough. Now do me a favor and go home. I have plenty of things to do, and you've already wasted far too much of my time!"
Thalìa stared at her, shocked—her aunt had never spoken to her so rudely before.
"But..." she tried to respond.
"No buts. Go."
Shut out with no chance to argue further, Thalìa stood and left.

CHAPTER 9

Thalìa had been so upset that she hadn't dared to ask her aunt—or anyone else—about the castle again.

She locked her curiosity away in her heart, telling herself that one day, when she was older, she would uncover everything on her own.

And so, ten years passed.

Thalìa grew into a young woman of eighteen, with rare, delicate beauty. Her long, luminous blonde curls cascaded down her back, and her eyes were a striking, deep blue. She had a strong-willed character, having kept the adventurous spirit of her childhood intact.

Even now, just as back then, she wasn't very popular among her peers.

She always spoke her mind, refused to conform, and much preferred running or spending long hours reading adventurous stories to sitting and embroidering or trying on dresses like the other girls in Iontach.

That day, while waiting for the school bell to ring and signal the start of class, she sat on the outer wall of the school, listening to some of her classmates.

Susanne, Danielle, Estrella, and Julienne were the complete opposite of Thalìa.

Extremely conceited, they were convinced they were the four most beautiful and sought-after girls in Iontach.

"...and so, for my birthday, Mom is throwing me a party! It's going to be amazing! You'll all come, right? All the best suitors in town will be there!" Susanne announced proudly.

Thalìa couldn't resist responding.

"Oh, of course... wouldn't want to miss such a monumental event..."

"You're just jealous!" Danielle snapped at her.

"And jealous of what, enlighten me... This town is so small that we all know each other, every single one of us. We see each other every day. We know what we wear, how we walk, what we like. No surprises. Honestly, forgive me, but I really can't imagine who these so-called *'best suitors'* could possibly be!"

"What do you mean *who*? Our future husbands, of course! Who else?!" Julienne exclaimed, scandalized.

Thalìa chuckled.

"What would you even do with them? It's way too early to get married!"

"Too early? What nonsense!" Danielle replied. "We're finishing school this year, and I want to start working at my father's deli, get married, and have a baby boy."

"Me too!" chimed in Estrella and Susanne in unison.

"And me..." Julienne added dreamily.

Thalìa jumped down from the wall, incredulous.
"Come on, that's ridiculous! How can you even think about getting married and becoming mothers when you know nothing about the world? What will you teach your kids? How to chop wood and sew? Or how to stuff sausages and cook? Don't you have dreams? Real ones, I mean!"
The others exchanged glances before turning to stare at her as if she were completely out of her mind. But Thalìa didn't back down and pressed on.
"I'd like to... I don't know... be an archaeologist, for example! To learn about ancient, lost civilizations! Or maybe... be a pirate! And fight all my enemies with my cutlass! And then I'd love to travel and..."
At that moment, the school bell rang, and Susanne cut her off.
"Who cares what you'd like to do? You're so... what was the word you used earlier? Oh, ridiculous—that's the adjective that suits you best. A pirate... What a joke, like you're still eight years old! Anyway, don't worry—you don't have to come. You're not invited. Girls, let's go. I'm not about to get a tardy slip because of her."
Stiff as four poles in a grotesque parade, the group raised their chins, straightened their backs, clutched their books under their arms, and headed toward the stairs.
Thalìa, after a moment of hesitation, ran after them.

"Wait, girls, hold on!"
"What now?" Julianne snapped, turning back with an annoyed glare.
"I was thinking... what if we just didn't go to class this morning?"
Estrella stepped closer, intrigued.
"Let's hear it. What's your idea?"
Thalìa gave it a shot.
"I'd love to go to the castle! You've never been, but it's an amazing place! You'd love it, I promise!"
She said it with genuine enthusiasm, but the others exchanged looks, wearing the same disgusted expressions as before.
"That's what you wanted to say?" Julianne scoffed.
"If you want to go, go ahead. We won't rat you out. But we have way better things to do. Let's move," Susanne concluded.
They turned on their heels and disappeared into the school entrance, followed by a flood of other students.
Among them, a boy bumped into Thalìa so hard she nearly lost her balance.
"Move it!" he shouted over his shoulder.
She stood watching him for a moment, a frown of disappointment crossing her face. Then, resigned, she walked away.

That morning, she had made up her mind to return to the castle.
It had been years since she'd last gone, but for days now, she hadn't been able to stop dreaming about it.
She dreamed of strange, inexplicable images: a faceless boy running along a beach, dogs, a snow-covered park, two pairs of piercing blue eyes peering out from a hedge, a crying child, a grand ballroom filled with people and joy, a raging snowstorm... and a bloodcurdling scream.
And that's when she'd wake up.
Every time.
Restless and uneasy, but with a deep feeling in her heart that she had to return there, no matter what.
This time, she would follow that feeling.
She pulled a music box out of the pocket of her dress. At its center was now a young woman, identical in age and features to her. Winding it up, she set off toward her destination, running, dancing, and singing to the melody's tune.

On the beach where George had been living for eighteen long years, the sky was filled with dark, threatening clouds, and the stormy sea crashed its massive waves violently onto the shore.
To shield himself from the rain that would soon pour down, he had found shelter in a nearby cave, safely out of reach of

the waves. It was much warmer and safer than his usual refuge.

He looked around, feeling fairly satisfied.

He had prepared a comfortable bed, placing on it his constant companion, the frozen stuffed animal Ciùciù. He had also stocked up on plenty of provisions in case the storm lasted longer than expected... but one thing was missing to put his mind at ease: the presence of his dogs.

"Where could they have gone in weather like this?" he wondered aloud.

He stepped out of the cave and looked around, trying to spot them. When he couldn't see them anywhere, he decided to go search for them.

"Ellyyyyy,Ioooooo, Aleeeexx!" George shouted over and over. He was trying desperately to make himself heard, but it was nearly impossible. The wind howled so fiercely, drowning out every sound.

He kept yelling and pushing forward with great difficulty for quite some time, until finally, he saw them!

His heart stopped.

Completely oblivious to the danger, little Jo was racing like a rocket straight toward a wave as tall as the walls of Iontach Castle, growling at it as if trying to challenge it!

Alex and Elly barked frantically at the pup, trying to get him to turn back, but he seemed deaf to their calls.

Panicked, George sprinted toward the small dog.

"Joooo! Joooooooo!!!" he screamed desperately. "Come back! You can’t stop the waves—it’s dangerous!!! Jo, come here, Joooo!"

But Jo didn’t hear him and was swallowed by the sea.

George, too, was overwhelmed.

As he struggled against the pull of the current, trying to stay onshore, he saw Alex dart past him and dive in without hesitation to rescue his son.

George ran toward the water and dove in after them.

The wave hit him full force, and the undertow dragged him violently backward, slamming him against a rock.

He blacked out.

The torrential rain that began pouring at that very moment brought him back to consciousness.

Still dazed from the impact, he staggered to his feet and looked around frantically for the dogs.

Alex had managed to rescue his terrified son. Holding him firmly by the scruff of his neck, he was swimming toward George, desperately seeking help.

George rushed toward them!

He barely had time to grab the little pup into his arms before he noticed an even larger wave rolling toward them.

"Alex, run! Ruuuuuuuuuuuun!!!" the young man shouted, backing away as quickly as he could to avoid being swept away.

But Alex, exhausted and weakened from rescuing his son, wasn't fast enough. The wave hit him full force, dragging him out to sea.

He resurfaced moments later among the crashing waves, howling in fear and frantically paddling as the relentless water choked him, flooding his throat.

Under George's horrified, helpless gaze—and Jo's, who squirmed desperately in George's arms, trying to break free to run to his father's aid—Elly dove in, determined to save him.

She reached Alex and grabbed him by the scruff of his neck.

With resolve and incredible strength, she began dragging him toward shore. But another wave crashed over them both.

Jo barked furiously at the sea, his cries almost drowned out by the storm, while George screamed their names through the rain and wind.

It was all in vain.

The two dogs never resurfaced.

CHAPTER 10

Thalìa had finally reached her destination.

"Hello, Castle. I've missed you so much!" she declared, gripping the bars of the gate.

To her surprise, it was slightly ajar.

Excited, she pushed it open and stepped inside.

She moved forward cautiously, savoring the crisp, cool air that chilled her cheeks, while carefully taking in the vast park she had spent years trying to imagine.

The reality far exceeded her fantasies.

With each step, she felt as if she had entered an enchanted place, where every corner seemed to slumber peacefully under a thick blanket of snow.

It was like being outside of time and space.

As she wandered along the paths, weaving between the trees and what had once been sprawling green meadows, she suddenly found herself surrounded—escorted, even—by the animals of the forest.

Among them, a white cat approached her, purring softly.

"It's you!" Thalìa exclaimed, recognizing the kitten that had climbed into her arms years before.

"Meow... prrrrrrrrr..." he replied, rubbing himself even more affectionately against her legs.

She picked him up, and as if he had been waiting for that moment, he settled himself around her neck like a warm, fluffy scarf.
"Just what I needed, thank you," she said, her voice trembling slightly from the cold.
Sliding her hands under his warm fur, she immediately felt much better.
Reinvigorated, she continued her walk with her old friend and the other little forest creatures by her side.

Back at the wide beach, the rain had stopped falling; the sky had cleared, and the sea had almost completely calmed.
George, who had dived in once more in a final, desperate attempt to find Elly and Alex, resurfaced alone, feeling utterly powerless.
When Jo saw him return to shore with tears streaming down his face, he understood. The little dog let out a heart-wrenching howl toward the sky.
George tried to pick him up to comfort him, but Jo wouldn't allow it. Instead, he ran toward the sea, stopping at the water's edge. He turned his gaze to the endless expanse of water, as if hoping to catch sight of his parents' heads breaking the surface.
He stood there for a long time, looking in every direction, his heart lifting with hope each time a wave, slightly taller than

the rest, formed a crest… until, hours later, he realized it was useless.

Devastated, he crouched down and whimpered in despair, as large, warm tears rolled down his face.

George, who had been silently watching him, sat down beside him.

He wanted to comfort Jo, but he knew how pointless it would be at that moment.

There was no solace for the loss of one's family.

He remembered perfectly the day when, for him, everything had ended—or perhaps begun. That pain was etched indelibly into his soul.

He placed a gentle hand on the pup's small head.

Jo sighed and closed his eyes in sorrow.

A little while later, George spotted a tiny dot in the sky, distant at first but quickly getting closer and larger.

It was the robin, Picchi, darting toward him at incredible speed. In the blink of an eye, Picchi was right in front of him, flapping his wings frantically and circling George as if in a frenzy.

It was his way of saying he wanted to be followed!

George's heart began to race with joy.

"Picchi! Is it really you?! Where have you been...?"

But Picchi didn't seem in the mood to waste time. He circled George even faster, chirping more urgently than ever, like a whirlwind.

"Still the same old Picchi," George muttered to himself, feeling a comforting warmth and a renewed sense of hope.

"Jo, let's follow him, come on..."

The little dog, still sad and teary-eyed, reluctantly got to his feet and trailed behind them.

After a while, when they reached the cliffside, Picchi landed on George's shoulder.

"Why did you stop?" George asked, puzzled.

The little bird, unfazed, began to sing a melodic tune.

Suddenly, a powerful, blinding white light enveloped them.

As it gradually faded, in its place appeared the small door through which they had entered so many years ago. It was open!

"Are you telling me... I can finally go home?! Really?!" George asked, his voice brimming with excitement.

Picchi didn't answer.

Instead, he took flight again, heading toward the door, pausing to glance back to make sure he was being followed.

George nodded and motioned for him to wait just a moment.

Then he turned to Jo.

"Come with me. There's nothing left for you here... you'll like it, you'll see."

And once again, Jo followed him. Together, they crossed the threshold.

In the excitement of the moment, George forgot that Ciùciù was still back in the cave.

What a strange, unusual, and overwhelming sensation it was to step back into his mother's laboratory after so many years. George felt his throat tighten with emotion.

Jo, meanwhile, had begun sniffing curiously around every corner. At one point, he barked, drawing George's attention. The boy went to him.

"What is it?"

The little dog was nudging an old canvas that had been left on the floor.

George recognized it immediately.

It wasn't just any canvas—it was the one he himself had thrown to the ground in a fit of anger so many years ago.

A bittersweet smile spread across his face.

He gently picked it up and placed it back on the easel; then he ran his fingers over the portraits of his parents.

"I miss you, you know? ... so much."

He sat down on the floor and closed his eyes, trying to steady his heart.

A warm tear slipped down his cheek as Jo curled up miserably on his lap.

George stroked him, and they stayed like that for a while, each wrapped in the pain they now shared.

Thalìa stood in front of a transparent dome made of thin ice. Inside, two young people who seemed to be asleep were holding hands.

The crowns on their heads left no room for doubt—they could only be the two monarchs she had heard about, King Alexander and Queen Eloise.

As she looked at the young Queen, Thalìa was struck—so much so that she froze in place. They were so similar, they could have been sisters.

"How is it possible that she looks so much like me?" she wondered aloud.

Puzzled, she pulled out her music box, making an incredible discovery!

The tiny figurine inside, while still bearing her likeness, was now dressed in the same garments Queen Eloise was wearing.

Thalìa wound up the music box.

That peculiar object, known for playing different songs that always matched its young owner's mood, that day produced a melody entirely out of sync with how Thalìa was feeling.

Instead, it played Queen Eloise's favorite song—the very one the orchestra had been performing at the Carnival ball when the tragedy struck.
Fascinated, Thalìa placed the music box on top of the ice dome and stood captivated, listening to the tune she had never heard before.

"But... but this... this is my mother's favorite song!" George exclaimed almost in a shout as the faint, distant melody reached his ears.
He shot to his feet and, after ordering the little dog and Picchi to follow, dashed frantically toward the laboratory exit.
Even Jo had perked up, running so fast that George, unable to see him ahead, assumed the pup had gotten far ahead. What he didn't realize was that, little by little, Jo had become fainter and fainter until he vanished entirely.
George kept running—up the stairs and through the hallways—until he burst outside into the park!
"Mom!" he shouted, spotting Thalìa from behind, swaying gently to the rhythm of the melody.
It had to be her, he was certain of it!
"Mom..." he murmured again, reaching out to touch her shoulder.
But when Thalìa, startled and a bit frightened, turned to

reveal her face, it felt as if a cascade of icy water had poured over him.

Overcome with uncontrollable rage, he began yelling at her.

"Get ouuuuuuuut!!! Go... awayyyyyyyyyy!!!!!!!"

Thalìa, seeing what appeared to be a moving statue of ice flailing its arms and shouting furiously, its face twisted in violent anger, froze in shock. Then, terrified, she stumbled backward, fell, and scrambled to her feet. She ran as fast as she could, slipping and nearly tumbling several times on the snowy ground.

In her panicked flight, she never looked back until she was outside the gates.

Only then did she stop to catch her breath.

"What *was* that? A guard statue for the castle? Ugh, how terrifying! I'd better get home."

Clutching her side from the exertion, still gasping for air, she made her way back to the village.

Left alone, George gradually calmed down and noticed the music box.

He picked it up and studied it, curiosity mingling with a wave of deep nostalgia as he realized how much the figurine resembled his mother.

He wound it up again.

A different melody emerged. It was beautiful but unbearably painful for him.
He looked around, lost. Everything seemed frozen in time, unchanged from eighteen years ago... even the tiered cake his mother had prepared for him was still there, preserved by the ice.
His gaze stopped on the statues of the Cook and Jacqueline. The two women looked aged. That sudden realization hit him hard.
Time had passed, but he had forgotten to live.
He turned his eyes back to his parents, and this time, he couldn't hold back.
Shaking with sobs, he leaned against their tomb.
"I've spent years thinking only of you. Since you've been gone, I've sunk into nothingness... It's as if my heart has stopped beating, as if my soul has lost its rhythm. I feel so alone, so terribly alone, but... I can't go on like this, right, Mom? Isn't that right, Dad? No, not anymore. I need to start living my life again."

The new melody from the music box, unusually louder than normal, reached Thalìa, who instinctively reached into her pocket to check for her own music box—only to find it wasn't there.
"Oh no! I left it back there!... What do I do now?!"

She turned toward the manor, biting her lip in worry and frustration.

There was no way she could leave it at the castle—it was far too important to her! Taking a deep breath, she steeled herself with newfound determination and headed back.

CHAPTER 11

Thalìa cautiously approached the gate and peered into the park, searching for the clown.

There was no sign of him.

Summoning her courage, she stepped inside.

On high alert, she made her way toward the spot where the ice dome was located.

He was still there, bent over his parents' tomb.

Trying not to make a sound, she hid behind a tree and took a moment to observe him more closely.

His expression was so melancholic that... *"Maybe he's not as bad as he seems..."* she thought.

Taking a deep breath, she stepped out into the open.

The sound of her footsteps snapped George to attention.

He lifted his head sharply and addressed her harshly:

"What are you still doing here?! I told you to leave!"

This time, Thalìa didn't back down. In fact, she stood her ground.

Cautious but determined, she stepped closer, her gaze fixed on the music box he had placed back on the ice dome.

"That's mine. I'm taking it back," she said, moving toward the toy.

George got there first, grabbing it and flashing her a mocking smile.

"Can something that's in my house truly belong to you?"

Thalìa hadn't expected that response, and it began to irritate her.

"What a ridiculous argument! I'm here too, but that doesn't make me your property!"

"Is that so? ... Or maybe it does?"

His tone was so menacing that Thalìa's confidence started to waver. Instinctively, she switched tactics.

"Come on, be reasonable. I just want my music box. Once I have it, I'll leave, and you'll never see me again... I promise!"

George turned the music box over in his hands.

"Why does it matter so much to you? It's just a toy..."

Thalìa weighed her words carefully.

"It's not an ordinary music box. There's something different about it... You could say it's *grown up* with me."

"In what way?" he asked, intrigued.

"Do you see the little doll inside?" she continued. "It looks a lot like me, doesn't it? ... Well... it always has! When I was an infant, it was an infant. When I was seven, it was seven... and so on."

"That's just a trick. Someone probably replaces the doll as you age to give you the illusion."

"It's not like that. I've thought the same thing in the past, which is why I tried to take it apart a thousand times! But it's no use. This music box is a single, solid piece. No one replaces the doll—it grows and changes on its own... and there's more. Even the music it plays is never the same; it changes depending on my mood!"

George looked at her skeptically.

"Are you telling me this music box is magical?"

"I don't know... maybe. My mother's dear friend gave it to her shortly before I was born. It's very important to my mom, and even more so to me. Please, give it back to me."

"I don't know. You didn't seem to take very good care of it, leaving it here."

"What are you talking about?! If you hadn't scared me half to death, I would never have left it behind!" she shouted angrily.

"There's no need to get so worked up. Fine, here it is... but don't come back."

"You can count on it!" she snapped, reaching out to take it... but as soon as she touched the clown, a shiver ran through her.

With it came a sudden wave of calm.

"But you... covered in all this ice... aren't you cold?"

George's expression hardened, becoming impenetrable.

"Keep your promise and leave."

The prince turned and disappeared into the thick of the trees. Thalìa stood watching him for a moment longer, then left. From afar, behind some bushes, two pairs of blue eyes silently followed her steps.

Seated on a high branch of a fir tree, well-hidden among the needles, George watched her. He was drawn to her, and despite himself, he smiled.

How peculiar she was, and what strange emotions she stirred within him! A bit of fear, perhaps, yes... nostalgia and... an overwhelming desire to know her and to... *hug her*. Hug her? Good heavens! How that thought had crossed his mind was a mystery to him, yet his heart wouldn't stop pounding in his chest!

But how could I ever do that?... If I held her close, she'd freeze... he thought with a hint of sadness, wrapping his arms around himself.

At that moment, as if it had read his mind, a little squirrel leapt into his lap, rubbed against him with cheerful squeaks, and gave his face a playful lick, inviting him to join in its games.

It seems this squirrel doesn't feel cold... he observed, surprised.

From that moment, the prince's mood shifted, and a new hope began to bloom inside him.

After all, if he had managed to survive all those years on a deserted beach, and somehow, in the end, had found his way back home... *maybe* the secret hope now hidden in his heart—to meet that young woman again, to get closer to her... and perhaps, over time, to *love her*... to love her and become one with her, as his mother and father had been... *maybe*... even if he'd only seen her for a few moments, even if the mere thought seemed absurd... it wasn't entirely impossible that it could come true!

George climbed down from the tree and began running and jumping through the snow, playing with the squirrel and all the other woodland creatures until, exhausted and content, he lay down on the bright, snowy meadow, surrendering to a restful sleep.

And he dreamed... as he couldn't remember having done since childhood...

There was the blonde girl he had seen earlier, and there he was, for the first time in years, wearing normal clothes. They chased each other through the fields, laughing and laughing as they hid behind piles of leaves or massive tree trunks, only to find one another again and resume their carefree game.

As they ran, the world around them began to blur, and they found themselves playing among stars and planets.

A solid current of air, like a pathway, passed nearby. Hand in hand, they leapt onto it! The current carried them through valleys and streams, over snowy mountains and sunny beaches, before gently setting them down on a vast, colorful meadow.

The meadow was vibrant with bright flowers and teeming with animals of every kind... ladybugs flying alongside large, colorful butterflies, blades of grass intertwining, and the two of them, still hand in hand, performing a silly dance before tumbling into the grass, springing up suddenly, and resuming their chase!

When they reached a majestic boulder, George climbed up and sat on it like a king on his throne. Then, he extended his hand to the girl. She accepted the invitation and sat beside him, solemnly, as though she were his queen.

Two little birds then perched on their heads, placing delicate crowns of flowers upon them.

The two stared at each other intensely for a moment. Then, overcome by a shy and gentle embarrassment, they leapt off the boulder together and began running again.

They stopped, standing face to face, panting and with playful, competitive grins.

George bolted toward a pine tree.

"I bet I'll reach the tree first!" he shouted.

Her cheeks flushed, the girl ran even faster, trying to overtake him.

"No, I will!"

The race was on, wild and unrestrained!

As they ran, they became children again—seven years old, or maybe a bit older—and the excitement of the game grew even more.

"Me! I'm going to win!" George shouted.

"No, I will!" she retorted.

They reached the tree at the exact same moment, panting, and threw their arms around it, holding it tightly as they transformed back into adults.

They gazed deeply into each other's eyes—so deeply that George, a little awkwardly, tried to brush her face with his hand. But she didn't let him. Laughing, she started running again.

"To the lake! This time, I'll win!"

George accepted the challenge, chasing after her with all his might.

But she was so far ahead, she seemed unreachable.

A wave of panic gripped George.

He pushed himself to run faster and faster... until, just as he thought he was out of breath and would never catch up to her, he saw her again.

She was dancing barefoot in the grass, accompanied by two playful squirrels that occasionally scampered up her, making her laugh uncontrollably.
Relieved, his heart dancing along with her, George watched her, enchanted.
Her laughter was like a cascade of crystal-clear water; her eyes, shining stars; her hair, a waterfall of pure gold.
He moved to join her, but as soon as she saw him, she took off running again.
Once more, he chased after her.
Just as he was about to catch her, he tripped, falling onto her, and the two of them tumbled down a grassy slope.
With swarms of butterflies and fluffy dandelion seeds filling the air, they ended up tangled together, holding each other close, faces flushed and gazes soft.
George stood up and offered her his hand to help her up. Then he stepped closer. Their eyes were locked, mesmerized, and their gazes sparkled with love.
Slowly, with his heart pounding as if it might leap out of his chest, George brought his lips closer to hers.
Both of their cheeks flushed deeply, and they kissed.

George woke up with labored breathing and flushed cheeks.
What could her name be? he wondered.

Then he stood up and, with a pleasant flutter in his stomach, made his way back home.

Behind him, a patch of enchanted snow melted away, and a tuft of fresh grass peeked through.

CHAPTER 12

Anne and Louis sat at the kitchen table, sipping bowls of hot soup, though their worry was so overwhelming they could hardly taste it.

"I'm back!" Thalìa announced as she walked into the house.

Her parents exchanged a glance—relieved, but now also very angry.

Louis stood up, and as soon as his daughter stepped into the kitchen, he planted himself in front of her with a stern, threatening glare.

"Where have you been?" he demanded harshly.

Thalìa lowered her gaze.

"The school called to tell us you didn't show up at all today," Anne added, pressing her. "Thank heaven you're safe! Now explain yourself—what was so urgent that you couldn't go?"

The girl, still staring at the floor, sat down in her seat without saying a word.

"Well?! Speak!"

Louis, losing his patience, slammed his fist on the table so hard that the bowls jumped.

Soup spilled everywhere, and Thalìa timidly lifted her eyes to meet his.

"... To the castle," she muttered.

If Louis had been angry before, now his face turned beet red.

"I knew it! That's it—enough with this castle nonsense! Fine, since you can't understand, your freedom is over! From now on, you're not going anywhere alone except to school! And either your mother or I will take you there every single time!"
Thalìa was stunned.
She found the punishment so unfair that she dropped all hesitation and challenged her father by meeting his eyes directly.
"But why?!" she shouted, standing up.
"Because I said so! Now sit down immediately!"
"Because you said so? Is that supposed to be enough for me?" she shouted even louder, refusing to obey.
Anne, who until then had chosen to remain silent, stood up as well and turned angrily toward her daughter.
"That's enough! Show some respect to your father, young lady!"
Thalìa, realizing her mother wasn't on her side either, deflated like a balloon and sank back into her seat.
"But..." she tried to protest.
"Silence! Don't you feel any shame for your reckless behavior? Skipping school, disobeying, going to the castle, and on top of it all, speaking to your father like that! You're disrespectful! ... Apologize to your father and to me!"
"I'm sorry..." she murmured.

She felt as though her mother had slapped her, so she said nothing more and halfheartedly dipped her spoon into the soup.

But she wasn't hungry. The memories of that morning and the need to share them were overpowering.

All at once, she blurted out, "I met the Ice Clown."

Louis, who had just sat down, nearly fell off his chair.

"Who?"

"A young man who lives in the castle. He's dressed as a clown, and it's... it's like his entire body is covered in ice. But that can't be possible, right?..." she asked, more to herself than to them.

Anne dropped her spoon with a loud clatter and turned to look at her husband.

Both of them were so shocked that all color had drained from their faces.

Thalìa noticed.

"Mom, Dad... please, I need to know. Who is that boy? Why are you so afraid of me going to the castle? What is all this mystery surrounding that place?"

"That's enough, Thalìa," Louis reprimanded, finding his voice.

"No, it's not enough at all! There was also a... a tomb there! It was made of ice too, and inside... inside was a woman who

looked so much like me that it shook me! ... Mom... are you really my mother, or... or am I that woman's daughter?"
Thalìa hadn't realized it before, but that thought was tormenting her so much that her last question had come out in a trembling voice.
Anne quickly moved to reassure her.
"My love... what are you saying? No, of course not. You are my daughter—my beloved, disobedient little girl...! Eloise is not your mother; I am."
She hugged her tightly, and Thalìa seemed to calm down a little.
"Please, Mom, tell me about her."
Anne sighed, realizing the time had come to reveal everything, and prepared to share the entire story.
"Alright."
"Anne, no," her husband tried to stop her, but she had already made up her mind.
She placed a reassuring hand on his and gave it a firm squeeze.
"Yes, Louis, it's time she knew. After all, there's no harm in it."
"Oh, sure," he grumbled, annoyed. "You always do whatever you want anyway. But if something bad happens because of this, don't come to me. Understood?!"

"Something bad?... What do you mean?" Thalìa asked, confused.

"Nothing, your father is just being his usual catastrophic self. Queen Eloise was too kind for anything bad to be tied to her, but..."

Anne trailed off, lost in memories of that terrible day.

"But what?" Thalìa pressed, bringing her mother back to the present.

"Well... the morning after Eloise and Alexander died, something so strange happened that... A current of air arose... icy cold. Not here in the village, only at the castle. It was like... infused with snow, and in just a few minutes—maybe seconds, I don't even know—it covered the entire castle and all its inhabitants in ice! This fueled wild imaginations among us all and stirred great fear in most of us. Not to mention how much Evilia fanned the flames."

"Evilia, always the same... But how did it happen? What could have caused something like that?"

"No one knows... but it was terrible. Eloise and I were like sisters, you know? She was so full of life, always cheerful, generous with everyone... She couldn't wait for you to be born! There were still three months to go, but she gave me the music box, saying she wanted it to be your first gift... and that it would bring you luck. She insisted so much that I take it on the day of the celebration! ... I've always wondered if she knew, if she felt that her life was coming to an end... and I think, in some way, she's protecting you, because with each passing day, you're more and more like her. It's so beautiful and so strange to watch you grow. For me, it's almost as if she never left..."

Thalìa was deeply moved by Anne's words and wanted to know more.

"What exactly happened that day?"

This time, Louis spoke.

"What happened was..."

Meanwhile, George, realizing that Jo was nowhere to be found, had turned the castle upside down searching for him. When he couldn't find him inside, he began combing through the park.

Picchi followed him, as if trying to help.

"Now you need to explain where he's gone. He can't just vanish into thin air, right?"

The little bird chirped happily and landed on a tree branch, whistling.

George stared at him for a moment before sitting down with his back against the tree trunk.

He was disheartened, missing his small, lively furry friend.

"You're right, Picchi. He'll come back."

"... and that's everything," Louis concluded.

From curious, Thalìa now looked perplexed.
"I don't understand. All this secrecy for something like that? And besides, even if there had been some kind of repelling energy in the past, like you said, it's gone now. I walked in without any trouble—the gate was open."
"Really?" her parents asked, astonished.
"Yes... really. And you know what I think?"
"What?" Anne asked.
"I think... with all due respect, of course... that you and the other adults in the village should be ashamed of yourselves."
"What?" Louis exclaimed, leaping to his feet.
Thalìa didn't flinch.
"Yes, you should be. You all claimed to love your Sovereigns so much, and yet you let a six-year-old boy... six years old!... face such immense pain, all on his own? It's a miracle he didn't die too."
Louis and Anne were overcome with a strong sense of discomfort.
"Now the Prince George is grown up... but... but... ...of course! How did I not think of this sooner?!" Thalìa exclaimed excitedly.
"Think of what?" Anne asked.
"Everything started with that party, right?"
"Right," Louis confirmed.

"So... maybe... if we organize another party like that one at the castle, we could break the enchantment... and maybe George..."
"... could return to how he was before!" Anne finished, her enthusiasm rising.
"Exactly!"
"You two are delusional—it's impossible!" Louis interjected, trying to ground them in reality.
"Maybe, Dad, but if we don't try, we'll never know! Will you help me? Mom, please; Dad, come on!"
Louis paused, considering it for a moment.
"You said the repelling energy is gone?" he asked, looking at Anne, while Thalìa nodded eagerly, trembling with anticipation.
"Then, all in all... I think it's worth a try. We have nothing to lose, and at worst, things will stay the same."
Anne smiled and turned to her daughter.
"Yes, sweetheart, we're with you!"
Thalìa, beaming with joy, impulsively hugged them.
"This is wonderful, thank you! You're amazing!"

CHAPTER 13

The next day, after school, Thalìa wasted no time and immediately shared her idea with her classmates. However, no one paid her any attention.

The thought of hosting a Carnival party in that cursed place was already absurd, but the idea that Prince George could still be alive after so many years sounded like the wildest tale of the century!

"I'm telling you, it's true!" she insisted. "You can enter the castle grounds now—I've been there! And the Prince... he's covered in ice, but he's alive!"

"Sure, sure, whatever you say," Francis mocked her, his unpleasant demeanor unchanged over the years. "Let's go, guys. She's out of her mind. See you tomorrow!"

"It's true! I swear I'm not crazy!"

No matter how hard she tried to defend herself, the others brushed past her, leaving her alone and unheard.

Only two classmates stayed behind: Danielle and Estrella.

"So... Prince George is still alive... Incredible," Danielle said.

Thalìa brightened up.

"Yes, it's truly incredible! But it's the truth!" she replied passionately.

"And... what's he like? I've heard he was a very handsome

boy... and that the King and Queen were just as beautiful," Estrella asked.

"Well... I saw them in their tomb, and... they were more than beautiful. He's... definitely very tall. Handsome, I think? I'm not sure... he's so covered in ice that it's hard to tell. But yes, he seemed handsome."

The two girls exchanged a look and nodded in agreement.

"Listen, we're in. Actually, if you're free, this afternoon we could go to the storage shed my dad has up in the mountains," Danielle suggested.

Thalìa's curiosity was piqued immediately.

"To do what?"

"My dad stores the food he sells in his grocery shop there. I'll talk to him as soon as I get home, and if he agrees, we can go grab something special for the party!" Danielle suggested.

"That's a great idea, Danielle, yes! And on the way back, we could stop by my house," Estrella added. "I have a real passion for lights and decorations—I've got tons! Danielle's seen them plenty of times, but I'd love to show them to you too, Thalìa! I'm sure you'll find something you like!"

Thalìa was stunned.

She had never been particularly close to Danielle and Estrella; they were so different from her that it had always been hard to connect with them. Now, though, the fact that they wanted to take part in the planning and were eager to contribute in this way was amazing! It would make things so much easier and drastically cut down the preparation time. Plus, starting the next day, their support would help her convince the rest of their classmates.

"Oh, girls, thank you! I can't wait! Alright, if your dad agrees, Danielle, let's meet in the square after lunch!" she said, glowing with excitement.

"Yes, but apart from my dad, let's not tell anyone where we're going today, okay? I'll even ask him to keep it a secret so we can surprise everyone!" Danielle added. "Hands in!"

The three girls reached out their hands toward each other, sealing their pact.

"Aaaaaand..." Danielle said dramatically, lifting their joined hands into the air, "the pact is sealed!"

"It's sealed!" Thalìa and Estrella echoed in unison.

Then they went their separate ways, each heading home. As always, Thalìa ran off at full speed.

That same morning, Anne and Louis had also been hard at work rallying the other inhabitants of Iontach.

Anne at the washhouse, Louis at Fred the baker's shop—they had managed to capture the attention of many.

Fred, in particular, was the most enthusiastic. He had always thought Thalìa had something special.

"I'm in, by thunder, absolutely in! That girl is brilliant! And I think her plan might actually work! ... The hard part will be convincing that bunch of hardheads living in this village! But we'll do it, won't we?" he exclaimed, clapping a floury hand on Louis's shoulder and bursting into laughter. "I'll lend a hand!" he declared.

Just then, Anne and six or seven other women entered the bakery.

"So will we!" they announced.

It didn't take long to get organized, and soon, everyone had begun their mission of persuasion—Fred with his customers, and Louis, Anne, and the others with every friend and acquaintance they encountered on the streets.

Within a few hours, there wasn't a soul in Iontach unaware of Thalìa's plan.

By late afternoon, the three girls had been marching steadily for a couple of hours toward the mountain where Danielle's father kept his storage shed.

On foot, the journey was much longer than they had anticipated, and Danielle and Estrella—who weren't used to constantly running back and forth like Thalìa—were already tired.

Estrella, panting, stopped for a moment to catch her breath.

"Danielle, how much farther?!" she asked between gasps.

Danielle grabbed her hand and, summoning strength and energy she didn't really have, pulled her along.
"Not much farther, but you should really start training a bit! Come on. Thalìa, stop running and wait for us!" she called out, struggling to quicken her pace to catch up. "Look at how fit Thalìa is! Hurry up!"
Not at all pleased, Estrella tried to keep up with her friend's pace, but her legs were giving out.
"You'll see, we'll find everything we need for an amazing party! Dad said there's tons of fresh stock in the storage shed—just arrived this morning!" Danielle said to Thalìa, trying to make conversation to buy some time and catch her breath.
Thalìa looked at her with a radiant smile.
"Thanks, Danielle! Mom and Dad told me they managed to convince a lot of people—I can't wait to start planning! It's going to be fantastic!"
"Yeah... fantastic..." Estrella muttered, her enthusiasm now at rock bottom. "... But isn't it a bit much to throw a party like this for someone we don't even know? I mean... he may be a Prince, but to us, he's a stranger, right?"
"He's not *a* Prince, he's *our* Prince! So he's not a stranger at all. Stop talking nonsense and pick up the pace!" Danielle scolded her.
Thalìa smiled and stopped in front of the others.

"Come on, Estrella, just a little more effort—we're almost there. And you know... before he's a Prince, he's just a boy a little older than us. His eyes were so sad when I saw him... I think he really needs a burst of happiness! A party is exactly what he needs—I'm more convinced than ever!"

"And we'll throw him an unforgettable one!" declared Danielle.

"Yeah, yeah..." Estrella muttered unconvincingly, still out of breath.

Thalìa took her arm to support her.

"Come on then, let's march onnnnn!!!" she exclaimed cheerfully, and together, they resumed their journey.

They finally arrived at the entrance of the cave Danielle had mentioned.

"It's so dark in there. Let's grab the candles," suggested Thalìa.

The girls opened their backpacks, took out candles and matches, and lit them. With the path now illuminated, they ventured inside. The cave was so damp that Thalìa shivered from the cold. She stopped, pointing her candle in different directions to get a sense of her surroundings.

"It's really dark here, and there are so many tunnels. Are you sure you can find the entrance to the storage room, Danielle?" Thalìa asked.

"Of course! I've been here a thousand times. Don't worry—it's just down there. We'll be done in no time. Follow me."
Candles in hand, the girls followed Danielle through a tunnel lined with stalactites and stalagmites. The rhythmic dripping of water from the ceiling echoed with their footsteps, amplifying the eerie silence.
"Watch your step," Danielle advised as she led the way. "We're almost there... here it is."
Thalìa looked at her, puzzled.
"Here... where? There's nothing but rock. Where's the storage room?"
"Right beneath your feet. Look."
Danielle lowered her candle to illuminate a spot on the rocky floor. There lay a sturdy wooden trapdoor with a large metal ring, secured by an iron latch.
"And we're supposed to go down there? You're out of your mind—I'm not going!" declared Estrella.
"But... if we don't go down, we'll have come all this way for nothing," reasoned Thalìa.
"Exactly, a wasted afternoon..." Danielle grumbled, annoyed.
"It won't be wasted. Go on, open it—I'm really curious!" said Thalìa.
Danielle's face lit up with excitement.
With the others holding her candle for her, she slid the latch aside, grabbed the metal ring, and began pulling to open the

trapdoor.
Despite using all her strength, she couldn't manage to lift it.
"Uuuhhhmmm... goodness, it's so heavy! I can't do it! And to think Dad lifts it in a second," Danielle complained, panting.
"Let me try," Thalìa offered kindly.
Danielle stepped aside, catching her breath, and let Thalìa take over. With surprising ease, Thalìa grabbed the ring and opened the trapdoor.
"See? It wasn't so hard," she said gently to reassure her. "Do you want to go down first?"
"Oh no, I can't see very well, and honestly, I'm not as agile as you. You should lead the way," Danielle replied.
"Alright, follow me."
Lighting the way with her candle, Thalìa began descending the ladder. But as soon as her head disappeared below, Danielle sprang toward the trapdoor, slammed it shut with a resounding thud, and slid the latch to lock it.
Realizing what had happened, Thalìa was overcome with panic.
"Girls, what are you doing?! Open this up, there's no air down here!!! This isn't funny—this is not a joke! Open it! Open it!!!"

Thalìa's voice reached Danielle and Estrella, muffled but still desperate.

"Are you sure about this, Dani? I mean... this isn't a good idea, is it? What if she gets hurt? What if... she actually *dies*?! Oh, please, no, no, come on, let's let her out. Now!"

From below, Thalìa's cries and frantic banging on the trapdoor could be heard. She was in tears, pounding her fists against the wood.

Danielle, consumed with excitement, seemed entirely out of control. She had achieved her goal.

"Let's hope she does die! If Heaven grants us this, we'll finally be rid of her. Come on, let's go!"

"Danielle, what are you saying? What has she ever done to us, really? Come on, don't be like this. She's right—this isn't funny. And you need to help me because there's no way I can open that trapdoor by myself!"

Danielle turned to her, her gaze icy.

"Do you want to end up down there with her?"

Her tone was so cold and menacing, more serious than Estrella had ever heard, that for the first time, she didn't dare argue. Fear gripped her.

Taking advantage of her friend's hesitation, Danielle grabbed her hand and began dragging her out of the cave.

"Let's go! And do exactly as I say, just like we agreed, if you don't want to end up like her!"

CHAPTER 14

Thalìa, surrounded by pitch darkness illuminated only by the faint glow of her candle, kept pounding desperately against the wooden trapdoor.

"Open up! Open up! Don't leave me here!" she cried, breaking into a fit of despairing sobs. "Don't leave me here..."

She wasn't the type to give up without a fight. After calming herself a little, she wiped her tears and began searching for an escape.

But there wasn't one.

She was trapped in a tiny, empty niche with a low ceiling and no openings apart from the trapdoor above her.

As soon as she realized this, a wave of panic swept over her, and she began breathing heavily, desperately trying to take in as much air as possible.

"I need to calm down... or... soon... the air will run out, and I'll die here... suffocating. Please, let Mom and Dad find me... Mom, Dad, help me... help meeeeeee!!!"

Her cries echoed hollowly in the desolate space, filling her with despair, and then faded into silence.

No one would hear her.

Exhausted from the long walk and overcome with fear, she slumped against the rocky wall and hugged herself tightly.

"It's so cold... so very cold..."

She began to shiver.

Danielle and Estrella were running toward the village; Estrella was trying to resist, attempting to pull Danielle back, while Danielle dragged her forward with force.
"Danielle, stop!" Estrella shouted at one point. "There's no air down there! I can't believe you actually want Thalìa to die! Stop this madness and let's go back!"
Danielle reacted poorly.
She pulled out a small knife from her pocket and lunged at Estrella.
"You need to shut up!!! And make sure you don't say anything to anyone, or I swear I'll make you suffer the same fate!"
The blade nicked Estrella's neck, drawing blood. At that point, terrified, she chose to comply.
Danielle yanked her even harder, and without caring about her friend's exhaustion, forced her to run at a relentless pace.

The village was abuzz with activity.
By now, everyone had been roped into preparing for the party, even the most reluctant of the townspeople. Men, women, children, and teenagers were bustling through the streets, making decorations, preparing food, and setting up lights.

Seated on a bench, Anne and Aunt Beth were drafting the menu for the event, while Louis, Fred, and the other men were unrolling countless garlands and enormous spools of string lights.

Distracted by Fred and Louis's laughter, Anne looked up from the list and glanced around with satisfaction.

"It's been so long since there was laughter in the streets... it feels like we've gone back years, doesn't it, Beth?"

Beth nodded with a smile.

"Your daughter is just like her..."

"Yes... And I'd really like to know where she's gone! She said she'd be out with her friends, but it's already dark. She's never been this late."

"She'll be back soon, don't worry. Hunger doesn't wait," Beth joked, bursting into laughter.

Anne joined in heartily.

At that moment, Danielle and Estrella came running, out of breath, crying, and looking utterly distraught. They stumbled to a stop in front of Anne.

Noticing the strange and noisy arrival of the two girls, everyone turned to look, and the chatter in the streets fell silent.

"Mrs. Anne, Mrs. Anne, quickly! Thalìa...!"

"Isn't she supposed to be with you?!" Anne asked, alarmed.

Louis rushed over immediately.

"Has something happened to our daughter?" he demanded.
Estrella burst into tears.
"W-We... don't... don't know," she sobbed, feeling as if her heart would break. "She was with us, but..."
Danielle didn't let her finish.
"... but she wandered off suddenly, and we couldn't find her! We tried looking everywhere!" she said, glancing at Estrella for support.
"... but we couldn't find her," Estrella concluded between sobs.
The villagers of Iontach, hearing this, began to panic.
They had just started preparing for the party at the castle, and now the very girl who had spearheaded the effort was missing. It had to be the work of the same witchcraft that had frozen everything years ago!
"Enough!" Louis barked suddenly. Then he turned to the girls. "Where were you? Where exactly did she wander off and disappear?"
Danielle replied promptly, her tone unsuspecting.
"Near the sea. We wanted to take advantage of the beautiful afternoon for an outing, so we hitched a ride there with a family on a cart. Everything was fine until..."
Danielle burst into such a heart-wrenching sob that Anne hugged her tightly.

"There, there, don't cry, we'll find her! Louis, let's take our carriage and go! Who's coming with us?"

"I am!" Beth volunteered immediately.

"Count me in!" Fred exclaimed.

The shopkeeper Gretel also stepped forward.

Louis nodded and turned to the villagers.

"Everyone, help us. The more of us there are, the better our chances!"

From the back of the alley, Evilia emerged, shuffling past the others.

She was very old now, hunched over and unattractive, and her habit of seeing witchcraft everywhere had not faded.

"You'll have no chance at all," she croaked, reaching out her gnarled hand to grab Anne's arm. "You'll never find her... and if you do, the curse will fall upon our village forever. This time, we'll all become statues of ice!"

A wave of fear swept through the crowd, the thought of Evilia's words being true unsettling them deeply. But Anne refused to be intimidated and shook herself free with a sharp tug.

"Get your hands off me, you old witch! It's because of you that people believed so many lies for so many years! I won't abandon my daughter like I once did with Prince George! I was a fool to ever listen to you! Let's go, Louis, we've wasted enough time!"

Anne, Louis, Fred, Beth, and Gretel walked off under the concerned gaze of the villagers.
Evilia raised her staff high into the air and began twirling it, singing hoarsely in a dark, ominous tone. Accompanying her words with a bizarre ritual dance, she chanted:
"No, no, no, this won't do, misfortune and doom this tale will bring through! Stay here, stay safe, and the curse won't ensue!"
As if under a spell, the crowd joined in her singing and dancing, moving in a hypnotic rhythm alongside the old woman.

CHAPTER 15

By the time the carriage driven by Louis arrived near the Marina of Iontach, dawn had already broken.
The narrow, identical streets were bustling with noisy fishermen returning from their night's work and customers eager to buy the biggest and tastiest fish.
At the port, Louis firmly pulled the reins of his two horses.
Anne, not even waiting for the carriage to come to a complete stop, jumped down and turned to the others, clearly agitated.
"Let's split up—we'll find her faster this way!" she instructed, unable to keep still as she watched her husband tying the horses to the watering trough. "We'll meet back here at the twelve chimes of the bell."
The group nodded in agreement, each heading off in a different direction.

Beth, Gretel, Fred, Louis, and Anne spared no effort as they searched tirelessly for information.
They even boarded a few merchant ships that were preparing to set sail.
Despite their determination, there was no sign of Thalìa; it was as if no one had seen her at all.

"Are we sure we're looking in the right place?" Louis asked as they all gathered at the agreed meeting point at noon. "Maybe we've miscalculated. It's true that the girls were here, but that doesn't necessarily mean Thalìa decided to come back to the port. Maybe, when she separated from her friends, she went somewhere else."
"By golly, you're right!" Fred exclaimed. "But... if that's the case, where could she have gone?"
"To the castle?" Gretel suggested. "Maybe she went to tell Prince George about the party."
"No, that doesn't make sense. Thalìa wants to surprise him—she'd never do that," Anne observed.
"Let's head back. She's probably already returned home," Beth said pragmatically.
"Let's hope so," Anne sighed, her eyes welling with tears. "I feel like I'm dying inside. But why did she wander off?!"
Louis pulled her into a comforting hug.
"Darling, calm down. Beth's probably right—she's home right now, wondering where we are. Let's hurry back; it'll take some time to get there."
Feeling slightly reassured, Anne climbed onto the carriage.

The candle was almost completely burned out, its weak flame casting eerie shadows on the walls.

Thalìa had cried so much and tried so hard to break through the trapdoor that she was utterly exhausted.
Leaning against the wall of the cave, her lips were blue from the cold, and her limbs stiff from the dampness, she was overwhelmed by the fear that she might die there, never to be found.
"M...m... Mom..." she sobbed, trembling.
With the little strength she had left, she pulled the music box out of her dress pocket and wound it.
The melody that played was both haunting and sorrowful.
Following its rhythm, Thalìa tried to stay awake, humming along faintly.

George had searched the castle inside and out, thoroughly and relentlessly. He had combed every corner, both indoors and out, yet there was no sign of little Jo. Still, he refused to give up—he would find him!
Thinking the pup might have doubled back and somehow gotten locked inside his mother's laboratory, he decided to check there too.
"Jo? Jo, where are you? Come on, come out! Where on earth have you gone?" he called out repeatedly as he searched every nook and cranny.
As he inspected the room, a sound reached his ears.

At first, it was faint, but gradually it grew louder: the melody of the music box.
"But this...!"
The sound was eerie, heavy with unease, and dragged along like a weary echo.
George suddenly recalled the girl’s words: *Even its music is never the same—it changes with my mood.*
Something was wrong—terribly wrong. She had to be in danger!
And if that were true, he had to help her!
Forgetting all about the missing puppy, George bolted out of the laboratory.

Thalìa, utterly exhausted, closed her eyes. Her head tilted to the side.

The melody of the music box followed George relentlessly, though it grew weaker with every step.
Desperately trying to determine its source, he hurried to the gate.
He tried to pass through, but an invisible and powerful force hurled him backward, slamming him to the ground.
Undeterred, he got back up and tried again, tirelessly, over and over... but the result was always the same.
After yet another failed attempt, an idea struck him.

Abandoning the gate, he sprinted toward the woods, letting out a sharp whistle.

By the time Louis and the others reached the outskirts of Iontach, the lights in the windows were all aglow, and the streets were nearly deserted.

The rumble of the carriage wheels on the cobblestones, however, brought many villagers outside, including Evilia.

One woman, noticing that Thalìa was not in the carriage, turned to Anne with concern.

"You didn't find her?!"

"...So she hasn't come home..." Anne replied, her voice trembling.

The woman shook her head.

Anne felt lightheaded and began to faint. Louis caught her just in time.

"Anne, Anne, come on..."

She slowly opened her eyes and looked at him, dazed.

"What will we do without Thalìa, Louis...?" she murmured, on the verge of tears.

"Don't say that! We'll find her!"

Fred quickly took charge of the situation.

"Everyone, come out! We need everyone's help! We have to find Thalìa and bring her home!"

"Bring her home... the castle's magic is—" Evilia began, but Gretel cut her off sharply.

"Oh, be quiet for once! Thalìa is just a child, and she's missing! We need to look for her, not get lost in your foolish superstitions!"

"Superstitions I've always condemned," proclaimed Father Angelo, who had also arrived on the scene. "Let's move, then! And you too, Mother!" he added, addressing Evilia directly.

She sighed in frustration but, for the first time, nodded.

"Fine, fine," she muttered. "Nothing good will come of this, but I'll help. Let's get organized!"

CHAPTER 16

The villagers of Iontach had answered the call for help, and a flurry of activity immediately followed.

From their respective bedroom windows, Danielle and Estrella watched the commotion below, careful not to be seen.

Danielle, restless and beside herself, no longer knew what she truly wanted. She hadn't believed that Thalìa could actually die, as Estrella had warned, and for her—someone who had never experienced death—the idea felt abstract and distant. What she did know was that she hated Thalìa, who had everything Danielle had always longed for but could never have, and she wanted to make her pay for it.

Estrella, on the other hand, longed to rush outside and shout to everyone where Thalìa was. Yet the memory of Danielle pressing the small blade to her throat and the wild look in her eyes held her back.

So, she simply watched, prayed, and hoped with all her heart that someone would find Thalìa quickly.

In the streets, some villagers worked to wake the few neighbors already asleep, while others began organizing horses and carriages.

Father Angelo took charge of the situation.

"Nothing was found near the sea where Louis and the others searched. Let's explore the countryside, and if that's not enough, we'll push toward the mountains!" he commanded. Then he turned to Louis. "You and Anne should stay here and rest—you're both too exhausted."

Seeing that Anne still hadn't fully recovered, Louis reluctantly agreed.

With torches in hand, the men of Iontach rode out of the village at a gallop.

Meanwhile, the older women had gathered in the village square, forming a circle around Evilia, who was busy stirring a liquid in a cauldron.

The old woman began muttering something under her breath, her movements growing more and more frenzied.

Steam rose into the air, forming the faces of two white wolves with piercing blue eyes.

While the women let out terrified screams, Evilia stared at the apparition in awe.

At that moment, the two wolves stood before George.

They were enormous creatures, their appearance both majestic and ancient, and they regarded him with great poise.

He stood tall before them, speaking with respectful urgency.

"Protective spirits of this manor, I need your help! You, who know all and see all, must be aware of the young girl who came here a few days ago. I am certain she is in danger. The enchantment binding me to the castle prevents me from leaving to save her. Please, save her for me. Bring her to safety at all costs! I will guide you with my mind."
The wolves sniffed the air and, moments later, howled into the wind.
They gave George a gentle nudge with their muzzles before dashing out through the gate.
The Prince watched them anxiously for a moment, then sat beneath a tree to meditate.
Focusing on the melody—now barely audible—emanating from the music box, he thought of the girl who had captured his heart. Before long, his spirit separated from his body and surged in the direction of the faint cry for help, ready to guide the wolves.

The wolves ran swiftly across the countryside, Thalìa's face vivid in their minds, and the music of the music box that George continued to transmit ringing in their ears.

Thalìa lay motionless on the ground in the now almost completely dark cave.

She appeared to be asleep, but suddenly her body stiffened, and her soul detached itself.
Looking around, she tried to understand what was happening.
When she saw her own body lying lifeless on the ground, realization struck—she didn't have much time to return to it: she had to act quickly!
She moved toward the ladder, climbed up, and passed through the trapdoor in search of help.
She wasn't sure how she could communicate with anyone in this form, but she felt a strong energy in the air and trusted that she would find a way.
The two wolves, as though sensing her ethereal presence, climbed to the top of a tall hill and stopped.
After surveying the area, they howled in unison and launched themselves down the grassy slope, running tirelessly through valleys, forests, lakes, and hills.
As Thalìa's bright, glowing soul floated above them like a breath of wind, George's spirit rushed ever more urgently toward the cave, driven by the need to find the young woman who bore such a striking resemblance to his mother and evoked such intense, unfamiliar feelings in him.
While Thalìa drifted through the air searching for help, four blue flames appeared in the distance.

Drawn to them, she moved closer, but as soon as the two wolves materialized before her, fear overwhelmed her, and she fled in the opposite direction.
Sensing her fear, George quickened his pace.
However, her body and soul were now in two separate places, and the dual sensations George perceived began to diverge entirely: the body cold and lifeless; the soul restless and unsettled. Panic gripped him.
He had to hurry, had to act fast!
But she had strayed too far from where her body lay, and he could no longer sense her clearly... Could he truly save her in time?

Thalìa felt lost.
In this new form, she couldn't recognize the path to the village, and the overwhelming sense of being alone and adrift in nothingness wasn't helping.
Unbeknownst to her, as she wandered aimlessly and at speed, she was moving farther and farther away from George.
"Where are youuuuuuu???" George shouted with all the breath he could muster.
The echo of his voice reached Thalìa, causing her to stop abruptly in midair and turn sharply.

It was behind her—she was sure of it! And it sounded just like the Prince!
"Here! I'm hereeeee!!!" she screamed in return, distraught but, for the first time, filled with hope.
Eagerly, she rushed in the direction of the voice.
George began to run as well.

The two white wolves arrived at the cave and entered.
At the same moment, the two young souls found each other again, though still at a distance, facing one another.
Slowly, with hearts overwhelmed by emotion, they moved closer. George extended a hand toward Thalìa.
"Don't worry; everything's okay now. You're not alone anymore—I'm here with you," he said gently.
She reached for his hand, and as he pulled her toward him, he embraced her tenderly, as if shielding a precious treasure.
The moment he held her, everything became clear. He now knew where to take her.
Taking her by the hand, he led her with him.

Sniffing the air, the wolves had reached the wooden trapdoor and returned to their natural forms. Whimpering loudly to alert the girl of their presence, they scratched at the ground above her.

In that moment, the souls of George and Thalìa entered the cave together.

As they drew closer to the wolves, George noticed the apprehension on her face.

“Don’t be afraid; they’re here to help you,” he reassured her softly.

She turned to look at him, as if seeking further confirmation, and he smiled encouragingly.

“I have to go now,” Thalìa said.

He released her hand, letting her go.

CHAPTER 17

Thalìa, hearing the scraping of claws and the howls of the wolves, weakly opened her eyes. Slowly, but with renewed hope, she lifted her face toward the trapdoor.

"Help... I can't breathe anymore..." she whispered, her strength nearly gone.

Then she fainted.

Realizing what had happened, the wolves bolted out of the cave.

Now, their mission wasn't just to find the girl—it was to find someone who could get her out of there!

In parts of the countryside far from where Thalìa was, the men from the village, guided only by the light of their torches, kept searching tirelessly—but to no avail.

"Thalìa! Thalìaaa!"

"Thalìa, answer us!"

"We've searched everywhere; she's not here!" declared Father Angelo before swiftly leaping back onto his horse.

"We can't stop now. Let's keep going! We'll find her!"

He spurred his horse and took off at a gallop.

The others quickly followed.

In the sleeping village, only the light in Thalìa's room remained on.

Anne, sitting on the bed in tears, kept fidgeting with her daughter's favorite stuffed animal, while Louis stood by the window, gazing out in sorrowful helplessness.

"Anne... we have to trust them. They'll find her, you'll see."

She said nothing, but after a moment, she angrily wiped her eyes and joined him by the window.

"Louis, I can't sit here waiting any longer. We've rested enough! She's our daughter—we need to go look for her ourselves!"

"It's the middle of the night, Anne..."

"Exactly!" she shouted, losing control. "Can you imagine how she must feel? She's just a girl, and she's been missing for almost two days! Anything could have happened to her, and we're sitting here waiting! It makes no sense! Enough—you do what you want, but I'm going!"

"Anne, where are you going alone? Stop. Let's wait until dawn and go together."

Louis tried to stop her, grabbing her arm, but Anne jerked away from him.

"Let me go! I'm not waiting for any dawn—I'm going now!"

At that moment, a loud scratching noise came from the entrance, pulling their attention away. They exchanged a glance; Anne's face lit up.
"Could it be her?" she said, rushing down the stairs.
Her husband followed close behind.

Anne flung the door open.
"Thalìa!"
Standing before her and Louis were two wolves.
Louis immediately grabbed a stick and moved to shield his wife.
"Careful, Anne—they could be dangerous!"
But the wolves did something unexpected—they bowed before them, as if trying to reassure them.
Then they locked eyes with the couple.
Sensing their fear, the wolves cautiously took a step closer before turning toward the road and stopping to look back at them.
When the humans didn't react, the wolves returned, studying them intently, as if trying to instill a sense of calm.
"They want us to follow them," Anne said.
Louis nodded.
"Let's get the horses!"

The few villagers who hadn't joined the search for Thalìa, drawn by the commotion, groggily emerged from their homes.

An old man in a nightcap stopped in front of Louis's horse.

"What's going on? Did you find her?"

"Maybe. The wolves want us to follow them!"

At that moment, the old woman Evilia appeared in a doorway.

"The white wolves always know the way," she confirmed with great solemnity.

"If that's the case, we're coming with you. Sleeping while your daughter is lost who knows where—it's impossible! Come on, everyone!" declared the man in the nightcap.

The others agreed, and soon, some on horseback, others in carts, another sizable group set off quickly, their way lit by large torches.

Ahead of them, the wolves led the way.

The final stretch of the night was spent in a frenzied race toward the Iontach mountain range.

At dawn, the wolves stopped in front of a cave and howled; it was clear they wanted to be followed inside.

Anne and Louis, without hesitation, dismounted their horses, lit two torches, and entered.

The others followed suit.

When they reached the trapdoor, the wolves began scratching at the wood. Anne, visibly shaken, quickly knelt down and handed her torch to Louis.

“Hold this! ... Thalìa... Thalìa?! Are you down there, sweetheart?”

“Wait, Anne, move aside!” Louis told her.

He broke the latch and pulled hard on the ring, flinging the trapdoor open.

Below, it was so dark that only a single stone step leading down was visible. No sound, just the rhythmic dripping of water.

“Thalìa! Thalìa!” Anne shouted.

“Are you there, little one?” Louis echoed.

Still, there was silence.

The two wolves pushed past the girl’s parents and descended below.

“I’m going down with them!” Louis said immediately.

“I’m coming too,” Anne added, but Louis stopped her.

“No, let me check if it’s safe first.”

With the torch firmly in hand, Louis began his descent.

“... Can you see her?” Anne asked immediately.

“Not yet. It’s too dark! Hold on!”

Just as Father Angelo’s group arrived, Fred and Gretel burst onto the scene, panting and out of breath.

“Well?” Fred demanded, elbowing his way through the crowd.
Anne looked at them, worried and speechless. She was pale.
Gretel wrapped her in a tight embrace.
“It’s going to be okay,” she whispered.

Reaching the bottom of the stairs, Louis heard the sound of the wolves licking something.
He turned the torch toward the noise—and finally saw her!
His little girl was there, unconscious, with the wolves trying to revive her by licking her.
Louis rushed to her, and the two animals stepped aside to let him pass.
“Thalìa! Sweetheart, sweetheart, answer me!”
He tried shaking her gently, but she showed no sign of waking.
“... Anne, she’s here! I’m bringing her up!” he called, lifting his daughter into his arms.
Then he turned to the wolves, who were staring at him intently.
“Thank you,” he said.
They bowed their heads slightly, as if to acknowledge him.

When Louis, followed by the wolves, finally emerged from the trapdoor, Anne rushed to her daughter. But as soon as she felt how cold Thalìa was and saw her so still, she panicked.

"She's dead!" she screamed, sobbing. "She's dead!!!"

The crowd began murmuring in shock and dismay.

Louis, who had heard her faint but steady breathing, quickly reassured his wife and the villagers.

"She's not dead! She's unconscious and freezing. We need to warm her up. Quickly, give me something to lay her on!"

Fred removed his heavy cloak and spread it on the ground, allowing Louis to gently place Thalìa on it.

Anne knelt down, cradling her daughter's head in her lap, while Gretel covered Thalìa with her own cloak.

The two wolves approached and bowed to Anne. One of them licked a tear from her face, as if to comfort her.

Anne, both astonished and overwhelmed, watched as the wolf that had licked her face began licking her daughter's face, while the other lay across Thalìa's body to warm her.

Suddenly, a man from the earlier search party, unaware of the situation, arrived brandishing a dagger.

"Watch out for those beasts!" he shouted. "They might attack her!"

Fred grabbed his wrist, forcing the dagger to fall to the ground.

"Don't be ridiculous, for heaven's sake! If it weren't for them, we'd still be looking for her! The wolves helped us find her, and now they're warming her. Calm down and let them do their work!"

The wolves, entirely unfazed by the commotion, continued licking Thalìa's face. Slowly, her eyes fluttered open.

Only then did the wolves step back, looking at Anne and Louis meaningfully, as if entrusting Thalìa to them.

"W... where... am I?" Thalìa asked weakly.

Anne threw her arms around her.

"You're safe, my sweet girl. You're safe!"

"But... how did you find me?"

"Thanks to them!" Anne said, her voice brimming with gratitude as she gestured to where the two wolves had been just moments before.

But there was no trace of them.

In the castle park, George opened his eyes with a sense of relief. Thalìa—that was the name he had learned—was safe.

CHAPTER 18

That morning, as Thalìa and the search party entered the central square of the village, the remaining villagers burst into joyous applause, and the bells began ringing in celebration!

Louis dismounted his horse and carried his still-weak daughter in his arms. Then he, Anne, and Father Angelo exchanged a knowing nod.

While Louis took Thalìa home, Anne, her expression serious, stepped toward the center of the square and climbed the fountain steps to be seen more clearly.

She then addressed the crowd.

"All right, all right, that's enough. You can stop applauding now."

Her words were met with compliance, and the applause gradually faded into silence.

"I want to thank everyone who helped us, but this matter cannot end here. When we found Thalìa, she was barely alive. If we'd arrived just a few minutes later... no, I don't even want to think about it."

Anne's voice trembled, and she had to close her eyes and take a deep breath before continuing. She then lifted her gaze.

"Where are Estrella and Danielle? I want to hear what they have to say!" she demanded firmly.

Father Angelo stepped beside her.

"She's right. Bring them forward."

From the crowd, Estrella's and Danielle's parents pushed their way through, their daughters timidly hiding behind them.

"What's this about, Anne?" Danielle's mother asked.

"Thalìa disappeared the day of their trip to the beach. What do our daughters have to do with this?" Estrella's mother chimed in.

Anne looked at them, her expression sardonic.

"Oh, *if* that were true, then nothing. But too bad it's not... isn't that right, girls? Your daughters, under the pretense of fetching food for the celebration, lured Thalìa to the old Storage Cave—the one no one's used for years because it's too damp, you know the one! They tricked her into going underground, locking her in one of the lower chambers, claiming it belonged to Danielle's father! Then, as if that weren't enough, they came back crying about her 'disappearance,' deliberately misleading us by sending us all the way to the Marina and wasting precious time! My daughter almost froze and suffocated to death because of them—*that's* what they have to do with this!"

A stunned silence followed Anne's words.

Danielle's father turned toward his daughter and her friend, disbelief, disappointment, and anger written across his face.

"What have you two done?! She could have *died!* Those storage rooms are cramped, cold, and airless! How could you even think of something like this?! How?!"

Danielle stood silent, her gaze fixed on the ground.

"I... I said it wasn't a good idea..." Estrella stammered, her eyes welling with tears.

Her mother slapped her so hard that the imprint of her fingers remained on her cheek.

"Silence! Do you really think you're any less guilty for this? You could have told your father and me the truth a thousand times since you came back. You could have helped the search and saved your friend! Instead, you kept quiet! I'm ashamed to be your mother!" she shouted.

Estrella, shocked by the slap and her mother's harsh words, couldn't stay silent anymore.

"You're being unfair! I never wanted to hurt Thalìa, and I tried over and over to convince Danielle to turn back! But she held a knife to my throat and threatened to kill me! Look! I still have the mark! ... What was I supposed to do? Let her kill me? Would that have been better?! ... Maybe it would have been better."

Estrella's mother fell silent, stunned by her daughter's words and the scar she revealed on her neck.

The girl continued, addressing Anne and the entire community.

"I know I made a mistake, and for that, I want to apologize to everyone. It's true—when I got home, I should have told my parents the whole truth, but I didn't. I'm so sorry, Anne, really sorry... but I didn't know how. I was terrified... I still am."

Her father, protective, pulled her into a hug.

Feeling safe now, Estrella turned toward Danielle, but her friend kept her eyes fixed on the ground.

"If things are really as she says, it's clear that the one truly responsible is you, Danielle," Father Angelo stated firmly.

"But why such cruelty?" Anne asked, on the verge of tears. "What did Thalìa ever do to you to make you go this far? Trying to kill her, threatening Estrella with a knife... why?!"

"She's different..." Danielle finally said, lifting her gaze. "She's not like us, not like me! She dreams big, and it always seems like everything goes her way! She laughs, jokes, plays all day long! And she questions the fact that Estrella, I, and the others want to get married soon and work in our parents' businesses! But what else can we do? Could we really become pirates, like she says? Could we really travel the world and choose to follow our dreams? NO! Because no one has ever allowed us the freedom to do whatever we want!"

"What are you talking about?!" her father interrupted.

"The truth! How many times have I told you I want to be a fashion designer and move to the Kingdom of Yaskà?! But I can't! Because you always said I'm your only daughter and that I have to take over the grocery store! Well, I don't care about your hams! I hate them! So if I can't choose my own life, then neither can she! Neither can she!!!" Danielle screamed, now hysterical and in tears.

Her father was speechless, and her mother was no different.

"And what did Estrella have to do with it...?" Anne asked cautiously, dreading the answer.

"Nothing. I just didn't want her to ruin my plan at the time."

Everyone stared at her in stunned silence.

Father Angelo was the one to break the unbearable silence.

"Danielle... it's true. Thalìa is different from you and from Estrella, just as she's different from me and from everyone else in this village and the world. But have you ever thought that you, too, are different from her and everyone else? I've known you all since you were little, and your uniqueness is what I love most about each of you. Being different from others is the greatest treasure one can have, but harming someone, even trying to kill or threatening to kill, is not the solution to your problems.

"If you have a goal, you must do everything to achieve it—through effort, driven by your aspirations and talents. If you truly want to become a fashion designer and you can't convince your father to let you continue your studies, ask for help from the community. Ask for help from me! I'm here to help every one of you. There's always a solution! Asking for help is not wrong; what's deeply wrong is taking out your frustration on someone else. Do you understand? Do you realize what you've done?"

Danielle nodded.

"Go to Anne and apologize."

Embarrassed, Danielle made her way through the crowd and climbed the steps to stand beside Estrella.

"I'm sorry, everyone..." Danielle said so softly it was almost inaudible.

"I didn't hear you, you disgrace to this village!" Evilia shouted. "Raise your voice like you did before!"

"I'm sorry, everyone," she repeated, a little louder.

"That's raising your voice?! LOUDER!!! Or I'll tie you upside down to the fountain and drown you with my own hands!" the old woman roared, her eyes blazing.

"*Mother...*" Father Angelo said quietly.

She turned to glare at him so fiercely that he fell silent.

Overcome by sobs, Danielle finally screamed, her voice breaking.

"I'm sorry! I shouldn't have done it! Please, forgive me! I'm sorry!"

Danielle's forced apology, however, failed to truly convince the people of Iontach. Many were still deeply unsettled by what had happened. Knowing that one of the village girls had nearly died over a petty act of defiance was far too serious to overlook.

“I can’t forgive you. I just can’t,” Fred declared firmly, standing tall in the middle of the crowd, his deep voice resonating. “Thalìa could have died. This can’t be resolved with a simple apology! Father Angelo, I demand that Danielle experience firsthand what she made her companion endure. I want her locked in one of our dampest, coldest, darkest cells, and she shouldn’t be freed until she truly understands the gravity of her actions. Only then will I accept her apology!”

Danielle was stunned; hearing such a proposal from kind-hearted Fred felt like a punch to the stomach.

His words didn’t go unheard. Even the village drunks, one known for his constant drinking and the other for his perpetual joking, supported him. Both had taken part in the search that day and, for once, were as sober as they had ever been.

“Fred is right!” they said in unison.

Shouts of agreement erupted from the crowd.

Father Angelo raised his arm to quiet the commotion and turned to Anne.

“What do you think?”

“I... I don’t know... I can’t think right now...” Anne replied.

“Then what about you?” he asked Danielle’s parents.

The couple exchanged a glance, both on the same page.

"Our daughter made a grave mistake. She needs to fully understand it," Danielle's father said, speaking for them both.

"If that's your decision..."

Father Angelo signaled to two guards dressed in black uniforms.

The guards grabbed Danielle firmly. Still in disbelief, she began kicking and screaming.

"No, noooo!!! Please, don't send me to prison! I understand, I didn't mean to! Mom, Dad, please!" Danielle cried.

Her father looked at her, disappointed, unable to speak.

Her mother's eyes welled with tears, but she stood firm.

The two guards forced the young prisoner onto a carriage equipped with iron bars.

One of the guards climbed inside with her; the other took the driver's seat, spurred the horses, and set off.

Danielle tried once more to cry for help and plead for mercy, but she was roughly grabbed and forced back into her seat by the guard.

As the carriage disappeared into the distance, a young man approached Anne.

It was Simon—the boy, now grown, who had once been Prince George's best friend.

"I have a suggestion," he said.

Anne smiled at him encouragingly.

Simon stepped up beside her, turned to the crowd, and after meeting their gazes one by one, began to speak.

“All of this started because Thalìa wanted to organize a celebration for the Prince and... well... given everything that’s happened, I think it would be a wonderful gift for her if we resumed the preparations and actually made it happen.”

The crowd didn’t respond right away. The idea wasn’t bad, but...

Evilia broke the silence.

“The girl is a friend of the white wolves. Nothing will ever harm us again! Let’s do it!”

A group of children began jumping and cheering.

“Yesss! Parties are so much fun!!! I’m going to dress up as a bear!!! ROAAARRR!!!” one of them exclaimed, imitating the big animal in a comical way and making many laugh.

“I agree as well!” Gretel said.

“And so do I!” Fred declared.

Before long, the crowd was swept up in a wave of joyous excitement. Anne, stepping closer to Simon, hugged him warmly.

“Thank you,” she said, her voice full of emotion and happiness.

“It’s my duty. I really hope Thalìa is right and that George can be saved. At last, I can do something for him.”

CHAPTER 19

George sat in the grand breakfast hall, perched on what had once been his father's armchair. His eyes were closed, and he was deep in thought.

"How is Thalìa doing..." he wondered.

He didn't understand the strange warmth he felt in the center of his chest every time he thought about her, but he couldn't help it—just as he couldn't help wanting and hoping that what had happened between them in the dream he'd had might somehow become reality.

Right now, though, he was worried.

He had seen her so pale when her parents had found her... it wasn't guaranteed she had fully recovered yet, and the thought robbed him of sleep.

The howl of the two white wolves startled him—now he would know!

He stood and rushed outside.

"Well?" he asked them breathlessly as soon as he reached them.

The two wolves circled him, nuzzling him affectionately. Before the boy, a white mist appeared.

Within it, Thalìa was seated on what must have been her bed. She wore a radiant smile and was embracing her mother.

George's face lit up.
"She's recovered! She's okay! She's okay!"
He felt more euphoric than ever!
Grateful, he vigorously stroked the majestic wolves' fur. After giving him one last solemn and reassuring look, they howled and disappeared into the depths of the forest.
As he watched them leave, George felt a pang of melancholy.
I wonder if I'll ever see her again...
Slowly, he returned to the castle.

In the tavern of Iontach, Danielle's and Estrella's parents sat silently stirring their steaming bowls of soup.
Danielle's mother, Anja, looked pensive.
It had been two days since her daughter was imprisoned, and neither she nor her husband had received any news about her.
"I feel terrible about what Danielle did to Thalìa, and I apologize for how she treated Estrella, but... I think my daughter wasn't entirely wrong," Anja said suddenly.
The others stared at her as though she had lost her mind.
"Don't look at me like that, Leonard. You know exactly what I mean!" she snapped, turning to her husband. "She's been trying to tell you what she really wants ever since she was little! Sewing and designing clothes for her dolls, making it crystal clear! But no. You—her authoritarian, despotic father

to the core—ignored her! Think about how our daughter must have felt, hating a classmate just because she had the freedom you've always denied her! It's you who should be in prison, not her!"

"Oh, so now you think what she did was justified?!"

"Don't twist my words! Don't you dare! Danielle was wrong—completely wrong! But what I mean is, if she did it, it's entirely your fault!"

"My fault, huh? Who told our daughter that if she didn't take over the grocery store, the only other option was to marry one of the wealthiest boys in the village and let him support her? Who?! Is that any less stifling? Go on, answer me!"

Albert, Estrella's father, placed a hand on Leonard's arm to try to calm him.

"... This isn't the place. You're making a scene."

Leonard and Anja glanced around.

Albert was right.

Everyone had stopped eating and was staring at them. Anja turned beet red, and Leonard forced a strained smile, lowering his eyes to his bowl.

"There's no point in blaming each other like this," said Rose, Estrella's mother, her tone calm. "You both made mistakes. But have there ever been parents who didn't make mistakes? We mess up all the time. The truth is... every parent tries to do their best for their children. But we often forget that the moment they're born, they're no longer truly ours. They have their own personalities, their own lives, and it's only right that they pursue their own passions, dreams, and ideals—not ours. We'll always be there for them, but we need to do so as silent parachutes, not gilded cages."

Leonard nodded.

"I don't want my daughter to be unhappy. So be it! When she gets out, I'll let her study fashion in Yaskà. The rest will be up to her."

"And who knows," Anja added, half-joking but with a hint of seriousness, "maybe in that big city, she'll even find a better match than the ones here..."

The others gave her a look. She burst out laughing, and her husband and friends soon followed.

Now that the atmosphere had lightened, they returned to their meal.

The village streets were alive with excitement.

The preparations for the celebration had now captured and involved every single resident—even the reluctant Evilia. Laughter, singing, and cheerful chatter filled the air.

The youngest children had a blast blowing up balloons into strange shapes and running from shop to shop, devouring the sweets they were given. The women were busy hanging garlands and sewing costumes, while the men sanded wooden planks to build tables for the refreshments. Musicians rehearsed endless melodies, and scattered throughout the village, other children and teenagers were engrossed in play.

The distant echo of contagious laughter and music reached the cell where Danielle was confined.
It was a dimly lit, small, stifling space—damp, cold, and silent.
Inside, there was only a wooden bench and a small table, nothing more.
Danielle, clinging to the bars, was trembling uncontrollably.
"P...please... l...let me o...out... I w...won't do it a...again," she repeated endlessly.
Exhausted after so much futile pleading, she collapsed to the floor, breaking into uncontrollable sobs.

In the bakery kitchen, Thalìa, busy kneading an industrial quantity of various pastries alongside Fred and Anne, was covered head to toe in flour.
"Mmm... what a delicious smell... the cookies are ready!" she said, noticing their golden color in the oven.
After clapping her hands together and sending up a cloud of flour—earning herself a half-indignant, half-amused

"Thalìa!!!" from her mother and a hearty laugh from Fred—she pulled the cookies out and immediately grabbed two.

"Here you go!" she exclaimed, blowing on them and holding them out. "Are they good?"

Anne couldn't help but laugh.

"Thalìa, at this rate, there won't be any left for anyone else!"

"Don't be such a spoilsport, Anne!" Fred said, reaching out his hand. "Hand one over, young lady!"

Anne took one too.

As they bit into the cookies, their delighted expressions left no room for doubt.

"I'll have to keep an eye on you, young lady! You might end up stealing my job, by golly!"

"It's true, sweetheart. They're amazing."

"Perfect, then!" Thalìa exclaimed.

She grabbed the entire tray, poured the cookies into a soft cloth inside a wicker basket, secured it, and then dashed out of the shop.

"Hey, where are you going?" her mother called after her.

"I'll tell you later, I've got something to do!" she shouted back, disappearing down the street.

"Are you sure?"

"Of course I am, Father Angelo. It's been two days already—I think that's enough time to understand, don't you? She risks getting sick, and I don't want that to happen."

The sound of their footsteps echoed through the prison corridors.

When they reached the area where Danielle was being held, Father Angelo motioned to the guards to let them through.

The guards complied, escorting them to the cell.

"Danielle..." Thalìa called.

The prisoner raised an ironic glance toward her.

"Did you come to mock me?"

"My name's not Danielle," she replied quickly, her bright smile lighting up the dim space. "I came to get you out."

Her companion stared at her in disbelief.

"How? Why? ... Don't you hate me?"

"Of course I don't hate you. They told me what you said, and... I understand now. I'm sorry—I didn't realize that being myself could hurt you so much. It's just that I can't help it—it's who I am! And sometimes, by only seeing things from my perspective, I act thoughtlessly. I'm sorry for how I behaved; I never meant to hurt you. Guards, could you please open the door?"

The guards looked at Father Angelo, who nodded in agreement, and they opened the cell.

Danielle stepped out, and Thalìa, ready, draped a warm blanket over her shoulders and handed her a basket filled with cookies.

"I thought you might be cold and hungry... Here, these are for you. They're warm, fresh out of the oven... and soooo good!"

Danielle took the basket, tears welling in her eyes, deeply moved.

That gesture taught her more than two days in prison ever could.

She threw her arms around Thalìa in an impulsive hug.

"Thank you! ... And I'm sorry, I'm so, so sorry."

When Danielle returned home, she learned that if she managed to pass the school year, she wouldn't have to start working in her father's shop or search for a wealthy suitor to marry. Instead, she would be leaving for Yaskà to fulfill her greatest dream!

Happier than she had ever been, her eyes sparkling with pure joy for the first time in as long as she could remember, she rushed to apologize to Estrella. Together with her and their other schoolmates, she joined in the preparations for the celebration.

As she worked, she thought about Thalìa...

After all, she was right: everyone could become a "pirate," ready to embark on a thousand adventures! This time, Danielle was ready to set sail and live her own!

CHAPTER 20

The sun, lazily peeking over the horizon, lit the path for the residents of Iontach as they climbed the hill leading to the castle. Dressed in their most original costumes, they followed Thalìa, who led the way with excitement.

For the occasion, Thalìa had donned a dress almost identical to the one Queen Eloise had worn at the celebration many years ago. The resemblance was so striking that she could have easily been mistaken for the queen, a thought that unnerved her.

... *What if George is upset by how much I look like her? What if he sees me as some kind of imposter and never wants to see me again?* At this thought, her stomach clenched painfully.

But as they reached the gate, her mind cleared, and her dark thoughts were replaced by eager anticipation to see him and surprise him.

If everything went according to plan, as she and the villagers of Iontach had envisioned, the Prince would wake to find the garden transformed into the vibrant, festive, light-filled scene of the celebration from years ago. He would hear the same music and feel the same sense of wonder.

Morning had fully arrived, and the gate stood wide open, as if the castle were waiting for them.

Thalìa noticed a group of children about to noisily run into the park.

Quickly, she stopped them.

“Wait, kids! Let’s play a game. If you can be so good and quiet that the Prince doesn’t wake up until everything is set up, at the end of the party, you can take home all the sweets you can carry!”

“Really?” asked a boy, no older than four.

“Of course. But you have to be very, very quiet. Can you do that?”

“YES! ... Ehm, *yes*.”

“Good. The game... starts... now...” Thalìa whispered.

On tiptoes, the children entered the snow-covered park, quiet as mice.

The preparations began immediately.

The children decorated the bushes with pieces of nougat, candied fruit, cookies, and all sorts of sweets. The men and boys assembled tables, lights, and garlands, while the women and girls arranged the food on the various tables. Finally, the orchestra positioned itself in the designated spot, just below the Prince’s bedroom window.

When everything was ready, and the Conductor was about to signal the musicians, Thalìa looked around. It was perfect.

She gave the Conductor a gentle nod, and with a sweep of his baton, he signaled the orchestra to begin.

The notes of Queen Eloise's favorite symphony rose into the air, the very same melody the orchestra had played on that fateful morning eighteen years ago.

George, deeply buried under his blankets, slept soundly with little Picchi dozing on the pillow near his head.

As the first notes filled the room, Picchi woke and began fluttering and chirping cheerfully above George's head.

Half-asleep, George tried to swat him away.

"Ugh... Picchi... stop... let me sleep a bit longer..."

But then he noticed the music and, astonished, sat up in bed.

"This music..."

His heart began to race, pounding wildly in his chest. His thoughts were jumbled, but a joyful and open smile spread across his face. With Picchi following, he dashed out of the room, down the corridors, down the stairs, through the atrium, and out the front doors!

The sun bathed him in its light, making his icy clothing shimmer like a knight's armor.

The people of Iontach held their breath, and the music softened, fading into silence.

The Prince found himself enveloped in an otherworldly atmosphere.

Before him stood a crowd of people, all dressed in strange, colorful outfits, staring at him.
Some looked astonished, while others greeted him warmly with nods or waves. Children gazed at him with carefree wonder and excitement.
In the crowd, George recognized Anne and Louis, their eyes brimming with tears, and he thought he saw Simon, his childhood best friend, on the verge of breaking down.
Then he saw her.
Thalìa stood beside the icy tomb, waiting for him. She looked directly into his eyes, offering him her brightest smile.
Struck by her resemblance to his mother, and with his throat tight from emotion, George walked toward her.
"Mother..."
Thalìa stepped forward as well.
Gently, she took his hand and placed it over his heart.
"Your mother is here now, and your father is with her," she said softly.
George grasped her small hand in his, then turned solemnly to face the people surrounding them.
It seemed as though everyone was silently encouraging him to act.
George turned toward the icy tomb of his parents and kissed it.
A single tear fell onto the frozen surface.

Slowly, the ice began to melt.

From where the two sovereigns had lain, vibrant, dazzling butterflies emerged, their wings sparkling in the light.

They flew around George, encircling him briefly, before taking to the skies.

Under the astonished gaze of the crowd, a powerful cold wind lifted George into the air, freeing him from the icy covering that encased him and gently setting him back on the ground—now dressed as a King.

The thick blanket of snow covering the meadows and trees, along with the ice encasing the castle and its inhabitants, vanished.

George stood in disbelief, overwhelmed.

He kept staring at his hands, his arms, touching his face to make sure it was all real. His gaze darted to Thalìa, who smiled at him with love, then to the astonished onlookers, trying in vain to make sense of what was happening.

From the castle doors, the servants of old began to emerge, stunned and amazed!

They had aged eighteen years, but their faces shone with joy.

Jacqueline and Adèl, finally reunited, embraced tightly, moved to tears.

Even Jo reappeared... though no one, not even George, could see him.

He ran wildly through the grass, barking happily, chasing the last colorful butterflies and soaring into the sky with them—up to where his mother and father were waiting for him.

Thalìa stepped closer to George again and took his hand. He turned, and without taking his eyes off hers, he took her other hand and gently pulled her toward him.

"Will you be my Queen?" he whispered shyly.

Thalìa felt her cheeks flush as hot as a roaring fire, her breath catching and her voice nearly failing her.

"Yes," she replied, not even knowing how the words escaped her lips.

George leaned in and placed the sweetest kiss on her lips.

The orchestra resumed its lively music, and all around them, the crowd erupted in cheers and thunderous applause.

EPILOGUE

The bells of Iontach rang joyfully.

It was a day of celebration. People laughed and chatted happily in the streets, and children ran aimlessly back and forth, simply for the sheer joy of it.

Picchi, his beloved Picchia, and their only chick, Picchino, flew from the bell tower where they lived, crossing the village, the fields, and the blooming meadows until they reached the castle.

Diving through the open doors, they swiftly flew up the grand staircase and stopped, fluttering, in front of a bright, transparent display case.

Inside was Thalìa's music box.

But now, it no longer held just the figure of a young girl resembling Thalìa. Instead, it displayed a radiant young queen, dressed as a bride, dancing joyfully with her young king. Above their heads, two adult sparrows fluttered gracefully, while beside them stood a pair of three-year-old twins feeding seeds to a very tiny sparrow.

The boy had black curls, and the girl had golden hair.

"Chichì, Chichì!"

"Here we are, Chichì!"

Hearing the twins' cheerful voices, Picchi and his little family settled on a beautiful brocade cushion to wait.

Moments later, like two tiny whirlwinds, Noah and Maryrose dashed toward them, hands full of seeds that spilled everywhere as they ran.

Thalìa and George followed close behind, noticing that their children's attention had already been captured by something else.

"Mama, Papa... a clown!" the siblings exclaimed in unison, their eyes wide with wonder.

George turned, stunned, and his heart skipped a beat.

Sitting in a corner of the grand hall, as colorful and cheerful as he remembered, was Ciùciù...

The little puppet, his companion during the carefree days of childhood and the darkest hours of adolescence, had returned!

His children had already snatched him up and were chasing each other, competing to see who could hold onto him.

George approached them and, with tenderness, took Ciùciù from Noah's hands. The boy stared at him in surprise, as did his sister.

Their father's expression was different than usual—it seemed distant, almost veiled.

George's stomach tightened painfully as a wave of emotions overtook him.

He remembered his mother's radiant smile the day she had gifted him the colorful little puppet; the comforting hugs

Ciùciù had provided during long, lonely days in the castle; the endless nights he'd spent sleeping with the puppet clutched tightly in his arms, while the dogs rested by the beach; the tears he'd cried into it...

How desperately he had searched for that beach again, but no matter how hard he tried, he had never been able to find his way back.

Overcome, George hugged Ciùciù tightly.

"Thank you..." he whispered into its ear. "Thank you for everything."

Thalìa, noticing her husband's unease, turned to the children.

"Kids, be careful. He's delicate!" she told them. "This puppet is very important to your father."

"It's true," George added. "If you treat him well, I'll let you play with him. If not..."

"No, no, Papa, we'll take super good care of him, we promise!" they interrupted, not letting him finish.

George handed Ciùciù to Maryrose, who gazed at the puppet with wide-eyed wonder.

"Go ahead and play, but remember what we told you," Thalìa reminded them.

The children nodded, each grabbing one of Ciùciù's little hands before running off toward the playroom.

As they disappeared, Thalìa embraced George tightly, and they stood there for a while, holding each other close.

“Are you okay?” she asked softly.

George buried his face in her fragrant hair.

“Yes, now I am.”

_ THE END _

ACKNOWLEDGMENTS

This is the very first story I ever created.
I was 5 years old, sitting at my grandparents' kitchen table, watching my grandmother at the sink, washing fruits and vegetables from the garden.
She was beautiful, my grandmother, with her black curls, bright dark eyes, and a warm, radiant smile... and she loved me so, so much.
As a little girl, I don't know why, but I was always afraid of losing the people I loved. Perhaps that's why, as I watched her, the story of George came to mind.
So, how could I not begin by thanking her? I miss her every day, in ways I never imagined.
Thank you, Nonna Rosa, not only for being moved when you read it for the first time after I wrote it, but also for always encouraging me. I wish you were here, along with Nonno Luigetto, to see how this old tale has evolved. But maybe, from up there, you already have...
A heartfelt thank you also goes to my mother. You read it when I was little, alongside Nonna and Nonno, and you were surprised and moved then. Today, you've read it again, with the same warmth and emotion.
Your enthusiasm, curiosity, and reactions have warmed my heart and inspired me with every chapter.

To RCP, my publishing house, a place that feels like family:
I want to sincerely thank the entire team that has supported me, and especially Roberto Calvo, the founder and CEO of this wonderful enterprise.
This book marks the beginning of our journey together… and it's so precious to me!
Thank you for your expansive and imaginative vision, and for the trust you place in me and my stories.
Finally, to you, my dear readers:
A heartfelt thank you to each of you who has read my book.
I hope I was able to take you by the hand and guide you into this new world. I hope it moved you, made you laugh, made you cry, and perhaps even made you a little indignant at times.
Sending you all a big, warm hug,
Len

P.S. If you'd like to write to me, stay in touch, and always be updated on the latest news, follow me on Instagram and Facebook at my username @eleanorlianofficial

I'll be waiting for you!!!

ABOUT THE AUTHOR

Eleanor Lian, the pen name of Eleonora Baliani, was born in Genoa in 1980.

From a young age, she loved devouring and creating stories, which she enjoyed acting out in front of the mirror. *I want a job that allows me to dream and share dreams for a lifetime*, she often thought. Continuing to craft stories—some of which she crumpled up and tossed away dissatisfied—she discovered her passion for acting at the age of twelve and began formal training.

Determined to pursue her dreams, she graduated summa cum laude in Performing Arts and earned a diploma in acting as well as certification to teach artistic subjects from the Achille Togliani Academy. Over the years, her days became increasingly creative and vibrant, filled with the development of new literary worlds, screenplays, stage plays, and acting roles.

With “The Clown and the Ice Castle”, she marks her third published work and her first international release.

www.robertocalvoproductions.com

@robertocalvoproductions

www.ingramcontent.com/pod-product-compliance
Lightning Source LLC
Chambersburg PA
CBHW020502310726
48979CB00016B/2762/J

* 9 7 8 1 0 6 8 3 0 8 9 9 4 *